Borne of the Deep

ADVANCE PRAISE FOR BORNE OF THE DEEP (THE SALEM HAWLEY SERIES, BOOK TWO)

"Edward Lee meets Victor LaValle for an extreme cosmic horror tale."
- **Scott Kemper, host of Staring Into The Abyss: A Podcast**

"*Borne of the Deep* is a bacchanal of myth, sex and gore doled out in equal measure. Hicks paints an unsettling picture—a dark and pitiless world of rot and monstrosities—into which he thrusts his steadfast hero. Infused with rich Lovecraftian imagery, imaginative horrors, and a wicked sense of humor, this entry in the Salem Hawley series grabs the reader by the throat and bites down hard."
- **Chris Sorensen, author of The Messy Man Series**

"The second installment in the Salem Hawley series picks up right where the first left off and moves at breakneck speed. Hicks deeper dive into the Lovecraftian mythos, and the addition of bad-ass heroine Louise LeMarche, ratchets this twisted, gruesome tale up to an unfathomable level and promises one hell of a finale in book three. I can't wait!"
- **Jeremy Hepler, Bram Stoker-Nominated author of *Cricket Hunters***

"Michael Patrick Hicks delivers a stunning follow up to *The Resurrectionists* with *Borne of the Deep*, a well-deserved update on Lovecraftian lore. Gruesome, repulsive, page-turning goodness! I loved it!"
- **Steve Stred, author of *Ritual***

PRAISE FOR THE RESURRECTIONISTS (THE SALEM HAWLEY SERIES, BOOK ONE)

"*The Resurrectionists* is a stunning achievement — an effective historical novel AND a brutal horror story. Salem Hawley is a fantastic protagonist I look forward to following in future stores."

    - **John Hornor Jacobs, author of *The Sea Dreams It Is the Sky: A Novella of Cosmic Horror***

"Grim, perverse, and written with literary panache, *The Resurrectionists* sets the bar high for modern authors of Lovecraftian horror. With its mix of Lovecraftian and human monsters, this opening chapter in the Salem Hawley series will delight readers of both cosmic horror and the morbidly beautiful works of Clive Barker."

    - **Glen Krisch, author of *Where Darkness Dwells***

"A masterful juxtaposition of human empathy with cold, ravenous destruction. The ending definitely leaves you wanting more!"

    - **Somer Canon, author of *Killer Chronicles***

"Gritty, grand and grotesque, *The Resurrectionists* is a mind-bending, Lovecraftian myth set in the murky underbelly of post-Revolutionary War Manhattan. It played out in my imagination in a palette of reds and browns like a lush Hammer horror film. Salem Hawley is a riveting avenger, and I'm eager to follow him on further macabre adventures."

    - **Chris Sorensen, author of *The Nightmare Room***

"As terrifying and action-packed as a slasher flick, but also saturated with literary merit at its core, exploring social issues like racism, classism, and the ramifications of medical experimentation. It was such a fun, provocative read. I can't wait to see what direction he steers the plot in the second book."

    - **Jeremy Hepler, Bram Stoker Award-nominated author of *The Boulevard Monster***

"A perfect blend of historical and cosmic horror. Hicks has definitely created something special here, simultaneously authentic and otherworldly. Great characterization, vivid

descriptions, and a cast of villains that will make your skin crawl."
- **Tim Meyer, author of _The Switch House_**

"A gritty, grisly historical fiction with poetic prose and plenty of heart and guts. A mesmerizing, cosmic horror tale channeling elements of Lovecraft and Chambers with a dash of Poe. I can't wait for the next chapter!"
- **Chuck Buda, author of _Tourniquet_**

"With echoes of LaValle's _The Ballad of Black Tom_, Michael Patrick Hicks's _The Resurrectionists_ conjures a unique and horrifying vision from the void beyond. I can't wait to see where the series goes next."
- **Todd Keisling, author of _The Final Reconciliation_ and _Ugly Little Things_**

"I had a BLAST reading this book. This novella captivated me from the get-go, introducing me to an array of characters that were fascinating in their own right. The last chapters held a special kind of mayhem, and I was in my element throughout."
- **Red Lace Reviews**

"One of the best Lovecraftian books I've read in quite some time. Fans of the sub-genre should find this book right up their alley... Michael Patrick Hicks captures the sense of helplessness, dread, and the smallness of Man in the universe very well."
- **Real Dead Reviews**

"Cosmic horror at its finest!"
- **Zen Bookworm**

"An intriguing tale of cosmic horror and grave robbing… a very entertaining read and deserves to bring the fiction of Michael Patrick Hicks to a wider audience."
- **Tony Jones, Ginger Nuts of Horror**

"To say that *The Resurrectionists* is a blast to read is an understatement. I devoured it in one sitting and the frenetic pace starts pretty much from the beginning and never relents. Hicks crafts an interesting mythology that permeates the story and this novel features some of his scariest scenes to date. If you dig cosmic horror and a historical backdrop, this is an essential addition to your library."

-    **Rich Duncan, Ink Heist**

ALSO BY MICHAEL PATRICK HICKS

THE SALEM HAWLEY SERIES
The Resurrectionists (Book 1)
Borne of the Deep (Book 2)

DRMR SERIES
Convergence (A DRMR Novel, Book 1)
Emergence (A DRMR Novel, Book 2)
Preservation (A DRMR Short Story)

OTHER NOVELS
Broken Shells: A Subterranean Horror Novella
Mass Hysteria

SHORT STORIES
The Marque
Black Site
Let Go
Revolver
Consumption

Borne of the Deep

The Salem Hawley Series, Book Two

Michael Patrick Hicks

BORNE OF THE DEEP
Copyright © 2020 by Michael Patrick Hicks

High Fever Books
First Edition: April 2020

Edited by Red Adept Editing
http://redadeptpublishing.com/

Cover artwork by Kealan Patrick Burke
http://www.elderlemondesign.net

Printed in the United States of America

ISBN-13: 978-1-947570-13-9 (paperback)
ISBN-13: 978-1-947570-14-6 (ebook)

For my wife and kids, always

Chapter 1

S NOW BURNED SALEM HAWLEY'S eyes as a small tornado of icy flakes swirled around him. He couldn't see or even feel. The numbing cold that froze him to the bone stiffened his muscles, making his movements slow and laborious. His stomach ached where he had been run through. An odd pressure was mounting across his torso, squeezing him so tightly that the stitches holding his belly together popped one by one. His hands beat uselessly at the writhing limb coiled around him, lifting him several feet off the white tundra. The tentacle slithered tighter and tighter, forcing the air from his lungs as it compressed him. His ribs splintered like ancient, dry wood, stabbing into his innards. He couldn't breathe, let alone scream, as he was crushed by the alien muscle. For but a brief moment, the snow parted, and Salem Hawley saw, far off in the distance, a massive shiny black pyramid.

Hawley's eyes snapped open just as he flung the bedsheets away from his middle. He had lost his blanket sometime in the night, and the top sheet had become twisted around his legs and stomach, cocooning him against the thin mattress. Heart racing, he struggled to get his breathing under control. His belly burned with pain, and the bandages around his middle were damp with fresh seepage. The bedroom's damp chill did little to soothe him as he tried to shake off the foggy memory of this evening's night terrors and the fresh thoughts of icy snow lashing his bare skin with a cold so pure, it burned.

The nightmares had been growing steadily worse and disturbingly more vivid over the last few nights. Always present were the images of snow, the mysterious pyramid, and those damnable tentacles coiling around his hips and chest, ensnaring his limbs in their vise-like grips. No doubt those awful visions, he decided, were the result of his ordeal at the New York Hospital, coupled with his late-night readings by candlelight of James Cook's adventures, all enhanced by a much-too-overactive imagination.

Damn it all, he thought, freeing his legs from the last winding bit of cloth. He stood to make water over his waste pot, and the draft from the window turned his skin bumpy with gooseflesh. The darkness outside was thick, the stars murky beneath a gauze of heavy fog. Sunrise was still hours away, but he thought it unlikely sleep would return. Staying awake was just as well, perhaps. He was to leave in the early hours with a man named Wright Post, a doctor and apprentice to one Dr. Richard Bayley, who was sending both men on to Arkham, Massachusetts, to recover a stolen volume. The book, an arcane and dangerous tome, Bayley had confided to Hawley, might have been responsible for the horrors Salem had witnessed at the hospital little more than a week prior. The occultists who had set loose the horrors that violated the city had fled north with this grimoire, an ancient text entitled *Al Azif*.

The monstrosities he had witnessed at New York Hospital were not ones Hawley was apt to forget anytime soon, regardless of how strong his desire was to purge them from his mind. Recalling the sight of many-fingered spiderlike abominations and the enormous alien crustacean that bit men in half sent a shiver through him more ghastly than the cold draft cooling his skin as he urinated. Although, truth be known, he would have rather faced off against those multi-legged albino creatures once more than endure a weeks' worth of travel north by stagecoach.

With a sigh, he shook loose the last few drops of piss and buttoned the fly of his sleeping clothes. He had yet to pack for the journey ahead, and set about planning for travel. He had few in the way of outfits, and they all went into a trunk, along with his stationery, writing implements, and several hardback novels, including Cook's *A Voyage Towards the South Pole*, *Vathek* by William Beckford, and his Bible. To the stack, he added the tonic Bayley had mixed for him to dull his pains, along with additional washcloths and bandages to keep his wound healing. He returned to his closet to retrieve his flintlock pistol and tomahawk, then recalled that both had recently been lost.

Both had been in his grip at New York Hospital, the flintlock raised to put a ball through that damnable crustacean's eye. Then the beast reared back, towering over him, and speared him through the side of his gut, hoisting him off the ground. Hawley had still fired, but once the creature released him, the hospital in flames all around them, he had lost his weapons, and very nearly his life. That he lived still was a credit to his friend, Scipio. Alas, the man was staying put here in Manhattan.

Hawley winced as he reached to the top shelf and removed a lacquered wooden box. Inside was an ornamental French flintlock. To his eye, the gun was quite ostentatious, with its gold and silver accents webbing the handle. Highly detailed carvings were even etched into the wooden body, around the golden barrel and silver flintlock assembly. The weapon ran counter to his simple tastes, but it had been a gift from a dear friend once upon a time. He cleaned the pistol, reseated it in its cloth compartment, and placed the box within the trunk. A pair of well-balanced, and quite well-used, bone-handle knives went in as well. After a moment of deliberation, he thought it best to keep one knife on his person, should the need arise.

He spent the rest of the early morning waiting for sunrise, reading by candlelight in an effort to distract himself. With each creak of board and every knocking noise of his apartment settling, he thought of those unnatural monstrosities and the savagery they wrought. He nervously eyed the shadows, studying the darkness for their creeping gaits and chittering maws. Focusing on Cook's words proved difficult, but he continued to try. Finally, at a quarter to three in the morning, a knock sounded upon his door. Mr. Post had come to collect him.

He and Hawley exchanged only a curt greeting, and Hawley was left to follow the man down the stairs, his trunk in tow, to the stagecoach waiting below. Hawley was grateful for traveling lightly, as he manhandled his trunk atop the carriage's roof. All he carried with him into the carriage was the knife on his belt and the blanket in his hand. The early-morning chill had seeped into his bones, and he covered himself as best as he could on the uncomfortable bench. Post, he saw, was already fast asleep.

All the better, then, he thought.

The carriage rocked as the horses set away from his apartment, the driver training them toward a northerly direction. Hawley kept his eyes pointed out the carriage windows, watching the shadows between buildings and the darkness of the alleyways they passed.

The confines of the carriage took its toll on Hawley's body, along with the jostling and rattling of the stagecoach over the uneven, muddy, and rutted trails. The thoroughbrace did little to absorb the bumps and swaying of the carriage's movements, and after only several hours of travel, Hawley already missed his relatively comfortable life in Manhattan, where all he needed was within reach of his legs. The flesh of his wound strained painfully against the stitches. Occasionally, a scab would pull loose and moisten the bandage binding his abdomen. The fresh blood, as little as there was, crusted, gluing the bandage to his skin.

Post spent the better part of their first day's travel ignoring him, refusing to exchange even a single word with a Negro. He slept fitfully, legs stretched out before him, as he sat on the leather bench opposite Hawley, wrapped in his blankets, until he grew too warm and wrestled them free in his sleep. Despite the ease with which he slept, Post awoke in a foul mood that further darkened the atmosphere of the carriage, his silence growing uncomfortably oppressive until he found sleep once more. Hawley knew, for his own part, that he would be sleeping little until exhaustion claimed him entirely.

After the middle of the afternoon, the carriage finally drew to a halt, and the men debarked to stretch—another painful moment for Hawley. When he raised his hands overhead, his gut threatened to split apart. The wince that creased his face was undeniable.

"Let's take a look at you then," Post said finally. His waved his hand toward the general direction of Hawley's belly. "Aldous," he continued, shouting toward the Negro stagecoach driver but not deigning to look at him, "why don't you scare us up something to lunch on?"

Moving closer to Hawley, he waved his hand again as if to magically raise the hem of Salem's shirt. "You then. Unbutton and let us get this over with."

Hawley complied, his eyes quite nearly stabbing Dr. Post to death.

The white man seemed unfazed, hardly giving Hawley even the least bit of attention. He pulled the stained bandages free and gave the wound on either side of Hawley's torso a cursory inspection. He pushed his fingers into the tender flesh around the wound, and Hawley, as he hissed through clenched teeth, caught the flash of a smile play upon the younger man's face. Satisfied, Post helped him rewrap the bandage.

"It looks to be healing well," Post said. "Now fold up the blankets and ready a fire."

Hawley seethed under the man's countenance, his injury seeping again from the man's poking and prodding. Teeth still clenched, he didn't bother to hide his anger. "Need I remind you, sir, I do not work for you."

"No, you don't. But you do owe a debt to my father-in-law, do you not?" Again, Post motioned toward Hawley's injury. "Consider this part of your restitution, unless you would prefer to forsake the carriage and reach Arkham under your own power, perhaps?"

Hawley's face burned. Post had him fit to be tied, and worst of all, the arrogant, pale-skinned bastard was correct in his accounting of the balances owed. Hawley did indeed owe Bayley for his medical services rendered, and the doctor had seen fit to provide Hawley with the stagecoach north, under the supervision of the man's son-in-law.

"It's quite a long walk, as I understand it," Post went on. "And there's all manner of trouble a person of your standing might inadvertently venture upon."

Before matters could worsen, Hawley turned heel on the man and set about folding their blankets, stacking them neatly on their respective benches. Once that was completed, he trudged deeper into the woods to relieve himself then to gather fuel for a fire. He neither heard nor saw any sign of Aldous hunting. The man was clearly quiet, an aspect Hawley was sure to be wary of, given the Negro's unknown loyalties.

Satisfied he had enough wood, Hawley returned to camp and got a good fire going, then he collected the necessary cooking utensils from the carriage's boot. He had noted a small creek flowing nearby and gathered water to boil for tea. Not long after that, Aldous appeared with two rabbits in one hand, his bow in the other, and set about skinning the animals.

Post, as Hawley had suspected, proved useless and pampered as he puttered around their small campsite to stretch his legs. In between, he spent his time reading within the carriage. Hawley noted the man had promptly unfolded his blanket and left it a mess on the bench when not in use. For a time, the good doctor disappeared into the woods and returned just as the rabbits were readied for eating.

The meat, Hawley had to admit, smelled wonderful, and his stomach gurgled loudly in appreciation. The fat on those small bodies popped and sizzled in the flames, leaving Hawley's fingers well-greased and slightly burned, despite the calluses marring his digits, as he pulled meat free of the bones to divvy between them. Aldous had made biscuits, as well, and cut off portions for the each of them. Famished, they dug in. None of the men spoke, their attentions focused squarely on the food before them. The only noises they made were minor grunts of satisfaction as they filled their bellies.

Once finished, Aldous attended to the needs of the two horses while Hawley broke down their small campsite. Post, he noted, was nowhere to be seen during these few minutes of activity but appeared once the work was finished and they were set to continue on.

Their journey northeast continued on in similar fashion in the following days, with the traveling companions speaking little to one another. On the third night, the hour winding toward the early-morning hours, Hawley, unable to sleep, unloaded himself from the carriage. The woods were pitch-dark, tree limbs reaching out overhead to blot out the stars and moon so that only slim streams of moonglow filtered down to the earth. His legs were cramped and achy, and he paced around the parked carriage to get the blood flowing once more, his blanket pulled around his shoulders to save him from the chill.

As he moved toward the front of the carriage, a soft rustle of cloth from the driver's box caught his attention. Aldous nodded, the whites of his eyes and the flash of his teeth barely all that was visible against the nightscape surrounding him. The driver held out a canteen toward Hawley, inviting him up.

Salem stepped up gingerly then settled in beside Aldous. "Thank you kindly," he said, accepting the proffered canteen, then took a small sip. He was unsurprised to taste rum, having smelled the liquor on the man's breath previously and knowing that many a stagecoach driver kept themselves warm in such a fashion.

"Have you worked for the Bayley clan for long?" Hawley asked, passing the drink back.

"Some odd years, yes, sir. Since the war ended."

"You fought, then?"

A cloud passed over Aldous's eyes, a sign Hawley was quite acquainted with. After a moment, the driver nodded.

There was nothing further to discuss in that matter, and Hawley understood all too well.

"And how is it working for them?"

"Same as any other job, I should imagine. You mind your business and do as instructed, and you find yourself compensated well enough."

"Same enough, indeed."

Aldous shifted uncomfortably, craning his neck behind them. Satisfied, he leaned in closer to Hawley, his voice lowered such that Salem had to strain to hear him when he spoke at last. "You'll want to mind your business carefully, as well, you understand?"

Hawley nodded once, briskly. He had resolved quite some time ago to mind himself around Dr. Post and to be wary in the man's presence. To have Aldous encourage his distrust was a sobering moment, and he wished to inquire further. Now was not the time for that, though. Not with Post resting against the other side of the wall at Aldous's back.

"Thank you for the refreshment." Hawley clapped the driver's shoulder genially and dismounted from the box. Continuing his circuit around the carriage, he stifled a yawn, pulling the blanket tighter around his trunk, and returned to the carriage. With Aldous's warning firmly at the forefront of his mind, he knew sleep would be furtive, it not completely elusive, yet again.

Chapter 2

A N OVERNIGHT RAIN LEFT a chill deep in Hawley's bones. The damp air infected the blankets and soured any efforts at keeping warm. To complicate matters further, the stagecoach had become mired in a shallow pool of muddy earth rising around the wheels, making it too difficult for the horses to unsettle the carriage. They were effectively stopped.

Without saying a word, Post merely looked toward Hawley and nodded toward the door. The message was clear. He was to aid Aldous in freeing the carriage. Keeping his complaints to himself and his face free of emotion, Hawley shed his blanket and ventured into the drizzle.

Although the rain had largely ceased, the air itself was wet, and the sky was a deep, threatening gray. More rain was on the way. Hawley adjusted his hat and moved to the rear of the carriage. Aldous kept to the driver's box, encouraging the horses to strain forward while Salem put some muscle to the rear of the carriage. The work was difficult, made worse by the slick footing. Hawley succeeded nearly as much in pushing his own feet nearly right out from under himself as he did in nudging the carriage ahead. His feet slid in the mud, even as he dug himself deeper and the sodden earth came up his ankles. Finding any sort of traction was utterly impossible. The earth sucked at his feet as he pulled himself free. Cold mud splashed against his trousers and slipped between his boots and pants.

"Damnit," he said, a bolt of pain spearing him in the middle.

The carriage rocked forward then settled back into its groove, accomplishing nothing. He put his back into it, his face screwed up under the exertion as he pushed. A muscle twitched uneasily at the base of his spine. Aldous shouted his encouragements. Whether they were meant for the horses or Hawley, he knew not. He focused only on pushing and the supreme effort of will it took to stay erect. His feet slid again, even as the carriage lurched forward, then his hands met only air as he fell.

The mud, freezing and wet, was jarring against his torso. His hands were buried up to his wrists, and when he pulled them loose, his fingers, covered in lumpy grime, looked positively deformed.

Slowly and carefully, he returned to his feet and made his way to the stagecoach, now several feet ahead. Shivering, he felt twenty pounds heavier beneath the coat of mud. At least he could remove his outer coat, but his trousers were a loss. With each step, he felt more mud sliding down the inside of his boots, slipping beneath his stockings and squelching against the fabric and soles of his feet.

When Hawley opened the door, Post merely looked at him, mouth agape. Then the doctor began laughing, making no attempt to calm himself. "My dear," Post said between convulsions, "consider the bright side, mayhap. At least the mud matches your pallor." Then he laughed uproariously at his own wit.

Hawley did his best to ignore Post's taunts, the knife in his belt practically itching for release. He wondered briefly if Aldous would support him in such an action, or if the free man was too loyal to his wage masters. Best not to consider it too keenly, he decided, shrugging out of his soiled coat and stowing it beneath the bench. His backside, at least, was not so badly ruined that it made sitting an uncomfortably soggy experience.

The bright side, indeed, he thought ruefully.

As he situated himself, the carriage began its forward progress once again.

"It occurs to me, we'll be arriving just ahead of Arkham's May Day celebrations," Post said. "I expect it should provide some welcome revelry."

Salem raised an eyebrow at the man, but said nothing. Indeed, what was there to add? He was freezing and covered in mud, and his unsympathetic traveling companion was ruminating on the annual celebration of springtime's return, of fertility and sweet young maidens dancing in colorful gowns, and ribbons around the Maypole. Although, he decided, a cup or two of May Wine, a lush mix of white wine, brandy, and strawberries, would be most welcome.

Post returned his attention to a novel he had been reading for several days, feet stretched out before him and crossed at the ankles. Hawley turned his attention to the window, studying the shadows lurking between the trees.

What little sleep he had managed to steal over nearly a week of travel had been haunted by visions of ice and otherworldly monstrosities. The creatures he had encountered at the hospital little more than two weeks prior occupied his thoughts and much of his attention, even in their absence. And now he had been tasked with chasing down the grimoire that had summoned them forth.

What kind of madness has ensnared me?

His mother, traded off by a Spanish landowner in Santo Domingo to a ship bound for the colonies, had spoken to him of vudú and magic. Throughout his childhood, it was common for his mother to carefully pass an egg over his entire body to absorb the negative energies around them and cleanse him spiritually. When he fell ill, she would place a bowl of salt beneath his bed to soak up the illness-inducing energies. She'd been a superstitious woman, but even in these minor beliefs, nothing she'd spoken of ever approached the madness he had witnessed. The unearthly creatures he had confronted were a far cry from the *loas* of his mother's vudú. Still, he had spent the days and nights since praying to Belie Belcan, the *loa* of justice, as well as Jesus Christ, for protection against the demons.

Thunder caromed across the heavens a few odd hours after their journey had resumed. The rain came, hard and fast, nearly blinding in its viciousness.

"Perhaps you would like to step out for a bath?" Post said, peering up from his book and eyeing his companion for a reaction. Hawley ignored him, and the doctor resumed his reading with a bemused grunt.

Truth be told, Hawley would have much preferred the cold rain to the hard crust that had turned his clothes stiff and cumbersome. His skin itched beneath the soiled fabric, and his feet, permanently cold, ached.

With the earth sodden, attempting a fire was pointless. The best they could conjure was smoke, and even that would not be enough to cook whatever animal they might capture. Post made the executive decision to skip lunch and press on with empty bellies. They did stop for a brief respite, their trail hewing closely to the banks of the Miskatonic River, to stretch their legs and empty their bladders.

Aldous was positively soaked through but made no complaints. He stayed with the stagecoach, presumably to protect their belongings, although the trail north had been rather desolate. Two days prior, they had passed a stagecoach heading south, but no other signs of human life had revealed themselves since. Hawley supposed there could be Indians in the area, but he had seen no evidence of this.

Hawley went into the trees to urinate. Long lines of rain dripped from the young growth in the branches overhead to patter atop his hat and shoulders. When he returned to the carriage, Post was still gone.

He gave the doctor several minutes more, thinking perhaps the man had lost himself in the woods to shit. He occupied his time by skipping a few small rocks across the river's surface. Small, dark shapes moved beneath the current. The frenzied, storm-churched waters warped the indistinct round shapes beneath. *Frogs, perhaps, or maybe turtles,* he thought. *Impossible to tell.* After a more than reasonable amount of time had passed, Hawley began to wonder, though, turning the matter of Post and his whereabouts over in his mind once again. When he looked to Aldous, the driver simply shrugged, slightly exasperated by the wait.

With a sigh, Hawley set back into the woods quietly. If Post had been taken unawares by something, or someone, Hawley saw no reason to announce himself. He also found little reason in perhaps startling the man and giving Post cause to shoot him. He stepped lightly, measuring each step carefully as he pushed through the forest's growth.

Foliage overhead bore the brunt of nature's assault, and while the rainfall was still loud against the leaves, it did not possess the deafening roar it carried from within the carriage. He listened hard for any voices, studying the ground for impressions of footsteps and broken branches that illuminated Post's progress through these woods.

Following the man's trail was easy. The doctor was careless or simply hadn't expected to be followed. He was not loud, but Hawley could still hear, if somewhat muted by the ill weather, the recitation of a foreign litany. The words were indecipherable to his ears, and he dared not approach too closely. Hawley pressed himself tightly to the trunk of a tree, peering out around the side of the thick, ancient trunk.

Post stood erect, head bowed, hands cupped together before him. He spoke and shook his hands, paused, then spoke and shook his hands once more. At the end of this litany, he flung his hands wide, scattering bones into the cold wind.

Hawley shivered as icy fingers crept along the nape of his neck. Post followed a more direct path toward the trail, while Hawley remained hidden from the man's view. Once he was certain the doctor had passed out of sight, he crept toward where Post had been standing, to inspect the ground. Small bones, most likely rabbit bones confiscated from their lunches, were scattered across wet leaves. From the number of them, Hawley suspected the man had been collecting them for the last several days, at least.

He grunted as he rose, his knees popping and aching from the chill.

Post glared at him as he returned to the trail. "No more dallying. Get aboard. We'll be late enough as it is."

Even as the hours rolled past midday, the skies remained nearly as dark as night, the rain a constant companion. Hawley dozed in fits and starts as he rested uncomfortably atop the bench. Post, as was his custom, napped soundly, apparently comfortable in spite of the accommodations.

Rain pounded against the carriage windows, and a blast of thunder startled Hawley awake, his teeth chattering from the cold of his dreams. As he so often was in his nightly visions, he had found himself stranded in a desert of snow. Arctic wind bit at his flesh and froze his eyes in their sockets. An impossible distance away, a massive black pyramid stood, visible only in rare snatches between the blowing cross-currents of unending snow. Dark and ill-defined shapes cut through the blizzard, closing in on him, their noises like the rapping of thick, wet fingers upon glass.

Several minutes passed, and still, the dread disquiet enveloping Salem Hawley did not pass. He resumed his vigil of the woods. The shadows between trees were unnaturally dark for the time of day and grew ever darker as the carriage drew them closer to Arkham. He studied the shapes, somehow darker than the darkness surrounding them, watching their movements. Fleet-footed deer shifted through the foliage, and the wind and driving rain disturbed the leaves, but little more caught his attention. The darkness grew gauzier and murkier as they neared their destination. Fog enshrouded the world as the woods to either side disappeared beneath the thick, misty blanket.

Intent on keeping their travel to six days, Post refused to stop for dinner, and they drew upon Arkham late in the eve with empty bellies. The small colony on the banks of the river was wreathed in preternaturally thick fog. Hawley could not recall a fog quite like it. Arkham was barely noticeable through the haze until they were upon it. Hawley could hardly see his own hand held before his face as they disembarked from the stagecoach.

When Post turned to him to speak, he had to raise his voice over the hammering pulse of the rain. "You'll help Aldous unload the carriage, and do make haste. I do not like waiting."

Before Hawley could even seek a reply, the doctor quickly put his back to Salem and strode through the mud. He entered the tavern beneath the lodging they would occupy during their stay. Aldous had stopped the horses as close as possible, but it gave Hawley some satisfaction to see Post's cape dragging in the muck as his feet sank into the soaked ground.

"I'll pass 'em down to you," Aldous said, stepping foot atop the side step beneath the carriage's entry. He grabbed hold of the nearest trunk's strap and hauled it over the railing encircling the stagecoach's roof cargo hold.

The brass railing and the trunk itself were slick with rainwater, and Hawley could hear the shifting of contents within the trunk as the top end lowered over the railing. A surprised look passed across the half of Aldous's face that was visible to Hawley as the unbalanced weight of the trunk slammed into his hands and upset his balance upon the side step.

Too wet to get a grip and his reflexes taking charge, Aldous turned his head just as the trunk crashed into the side of his skull. He let out a sharp yelp, then he was falling off the carriage step, down into the mud. The trunk fell free of the carriage. Its flat face landed squarely atop his midsection, where it stood upright and pinned him for a brief moment before gravity reasserted itself, toppling the trunk. It crashed top-side down, and the trunk's flat lid slammed into Aldous's face. The wet snap of bone and crunching of cartilage were barely audible through the rain. Hawley could only hear the unfortunate sound due to his closeness, but despite their proximity, he was helpless to aid the driver. His body was sluggish from exhaustion, his mind slow and left reeling in the wake of the accident.

Still, he grasped hold of his senses rapidly and went to work. The heavy trunk sat firmly atop Aldous's head, and Hawley had to strain with his legs to remove it. The sight beneath the cargo nearly made him wish he hadn't. Aldous's face was caved in, his cheekbones sunken to give his face a painfully deflated appearance. His lips were puckered open, just enough to show his missing teeth. Blood ran from his mouth and mashed nose. One eye had burst, leaving a milky film to trail down the side of his face. The other bulged from its shattered socket, unseated from its position in his head and cocked at a curious angle. A solid dent was visible on that side of the man's head, where the trunk had struck him in the temple. Given such a sudden and weighted blow, Hawley surmised the man had been fortunate enough to pass before he had even hit the ground.

Watching from the tavern's doorway, silhouetted in candle flame, Post shouted, "Hurry along with that now."

"Aldous?" Hawley said, eyebrows raised.

Post again put his back to Hawley, leading him up the stairs and to a room on the second floor. "In here. I'll deal with Aldous."

"What will you do with him?"

Post turned, finally, just inside his room as he waved at a spot against the wall for Hawley to leave the trunk. "Their local anatomist can make good use of the remains, I would imagine. That will be a matter for the morrow. In the meantime, the body can stay in your room. You'll lodge next door."

As he spoke, Post kept his eyes on Hawley, scrutinizing him with a wicked intensity. Eager to be free of the man's gaze, Hawley merely nodded. He was used to the judging glare of white eyes upon him. He was accustomed, too, to keeping his feelings invisible and lodged in a place much deeper than the black skin of his face.

"Sir." Hawley turned away from the doctor, closing the door behind him. Even through that thin barrier, he could still feel Post's eyes on him.

Cold rain had soaked Hawley so thoroughly that it seeped into his bones and made his teeth chatter. Even bundled in a blanket atop his bed clothes and with a hot pan having warmed the mattress, he could not stop shivering. The wet chill was simply inescapable. The cold, coupled with the agony of his reopened abdominal wound, made sleep difficult. So, too, did the dead body lying so near.

Aldous slept the eternal sleep on the floor, situated near the opposite wall, with his arms folded across his chest. Hawley wished he could have closed the man's eye, but the damage done to his face had been far too severe, and so he stared blankly from across the void.

Hawley had slept with the dead too many times for his young life. During the war for independence, death had been his constant companion. Through many a long night, the pained moans of the dying had kept him awake until he finally succumbed to exhaustion. Over time, he had grown so used to their ministrations toward heaven that blocking out their noises became no issue at all and he slept soundly through other men's pain.

The war was more than a decade done, and he had thought his time spent with the dead to be long passed. Ultimately, it was the quiet that kept him awake. Aldous's passing had come so quickly and unexpectedly that Hawley still carried some degree of shock over it. Perhaps if the man were gasping in agony, he might have slept easier. But the presence of a cool body, so near and so silent, left him feeling out of sorts.

He knew, too, what Post had in mind for Aldous's physical remains. The body would be sent to Miskatonic University, where anatomists would butcher and mutilate all that they could. Just some weeks prior, Hawley had stood watch in a graveyard to prevent the theft of corpses meant for such violation. He'd watched his friends murdered and attacked by grave robbers intent on unpotting remains meant for dark deeds.

The bodies had been used in an archaic ritual, the impact of which haunted Hawley's dreams nightly in some vague form or another. Surely the anatomists here were not embedded in the cult-like practices of their New York counterparts? But, then again, *Al Azif*, the grimoire used to summon those earlier horrors before one cultist fled with it here, had led him to Miskatonic. The book that the trio of travelers had been dispatched to recover, and already one of them lay dead in that pursuit.

Hawley shifted, wincing, his teeth clamped down on a scream. He'd put on fresh bandages, but the damage was done. Unloading his trunk from the carriage's rooftop cargo had been too much strain on the stitches in his belly, and the catgut had snapped, reopening his wound. The aches were the worst part. It only seeped from around the scabrous edges now, but the injury remained ghastly in appearance. He'd been only too happy to disappear it beneath a fresh cloth.

Lying there, he couldn't help but wonder what made sleep so hard to come by after so many exhausting days of travel, whether the cold, Aldous's body, the nature of their journey, the incessant pattering of rain upon the roof and windowpanes, the stink of damp mold perfuming his present lodgings, or the damnable swirling of his thoughts from one subject to the next. His mind was fleet-footed, jouncing along from one thought to another like the carriage over rutted road. Focus was as impossible as sleep, it seemed.

His thoughts turned as if on a loom, producing only the darkest threads. As he lay still, eyes closed and waiting for sleep, his mind drifted over the problem of rabbit bones and arcane rituals. He wondered what, exactly, Post had been up to earlier in those woods, what spells he had been crafting. And now, Aldous, lay dead and in repose. *Were these things connected?* he wondered. *Or perhaps, more accurately, was there any way they were not?* He imagined Post overhearing Aldous's warnings about the man, his pettiness getting the better of him.

And then there was Post himself. He, too, was an issue, with his pompous arrogance and open disdain for Hawley. Hawley would like to set the man straight on a few accounts, if only it wouldn't mean his own end for sure. Hawley doubted Post would need little in the way of an excuse to have him put in chains and whipped, possibly to death. Or, perhaps, Post had some mystic conjuration in store for his future. Perhaps the rabbit bones had been meant for him, and whatever dark sorcery was enacted to end him had yet to play its hand. Whatever Post had in mind, a punishment by the mystic or the mundane, only the merest provocation would do, and so Hawley knew his temper must remain in check, his tongue kept bitten firmly between his teeth.

Chapter 3

MORNING'S FIRST LIGHT BROUGHT with it a piercing scream, so shrill and loud that it shook Hawley awake, his muscles immediately tensing in response. His breathing grew rushed. He was on his feet in an instant, snatching the blade from beneath his pillow as he came to his senses. A bolt of agony speared his gut, and he clutched at his side, knife held before him.

Even in the dimness of the small room, he could tell he was alone. As the fugue of sleep dissolved, he realized the scream must have come from outside. Relaxing, he turned to the window and stared toward the alley below. He could not see much at all, other than shadows of people gathered beyond his sight, but the murmur of the crowd was clearly excited and tinged with an air of fright.

Quickly, he pulled off his sleeping gown and dressed in his day clothes. Fitting a black overcoat around his shoulders, he secured a flintlock pistol into the rig he had sewn inside the coat so that the gun rested comfortably between his arm and ribs. He slid one knife blade into one of the coat's side pockets and slipped a second knife into the belt loop of his trousers, hiding the weapon in the shadows of the overcoat.

He followed the noise of the crowd outside, passing by those few customers gathered in the tavern to break their morning fast. They chatted excitedly, with raised eyebrows or questioning looks upon their faces. Post was nowhere to be seen, and for that, Hawley was grateful.

Once outside, he gently pushed through the crowd, ignoring the profanities and curses directed toward him. Clearly, Hawley thought, whatever bastion of progressiveness toward the equality of men that was so famous in Boston had not yet reached the insular, backwater community of Arkham. Still, nobody attempted to halt his progress. As eyes laid upon the scene causing such consternation, though, he wished that somebody had at least tried.

Sensing his presence, a woman standing next to him with her hand over her mouth turned with wide eyes, as if to ask if her own eyes were deceiving her. Alas, they were not.

In the center of the circled crowd was a large baited fishing pot, the contents of which defied belief—or, perhaps, would have defied belief if Hawley had not seen equally frightening creatures merely a month prior at the New York Hospital.

Inside the pot were three pale, greenish-gray horrors. They were roughly the size of a young child, but hardly as innocent in appearance. Thick, interlocking scales lined their backs, and their bodies were crisscrossed with black pulsating lines. The creatures' networks of veins stood on end, giving the monstrosities a stitched-together appearance. Bipedal and with oversized, bulging eyes that refused to shutter or blink, they appeared trapped in a form somewhere between human and frog. Their hands and feet were webbed, each of the prodigiously long digits ending in wicked, curved claws. The noises their fish-like faces produced as they struggled to free themselves of the netting were plainly inhuman, like bleating croaks birthed from the dark hollows somewhere in their innards, and sounded vaguely threatening. They were talking, to one another or delivering threats to the assembled crowd Hawley knew not, and it sent chills creeping deeply through him.

"What are they?" one asked.

"Caught in this morning's catch," another said.

"Kill them," a woman shouted, hands cupped over her ears to block out the horrible noises of the frogmen.

Hawley studied the faces around him, searching for the fishermen. The creatures looked to be of sufficient weight, and the fishing trap was large enough that it must have required two, probably three, fishermen to haul them to shore and dump them here in the center of town. Had they left, and if so, then why? What rhyme or reason was there for this display?

Pressing through the crowd, a pale-skinned brunette approached. Curiously, her eyes were drawn more toward Hawley than the caged creatures. Her features were set in stone, betraying not a single trace of her thoughts or intentions. A cold wind blew the hem of her ankle-length shawl into a shadowy arc behind her as she strode forward to stand beside Hawley. She gave him a long, hard look, her eyes boring into the root of him, before turning her attention to the abominations before them.

The small frogmen bleated a shrill, piercing shriek as their long, thin fingers curled through the trap's webbing. The pot permitted little room to maneuver, even as they tried to shake their way loose, slamming their bodies into the trap and rattling it atop the soil. Mud stained their pale, white underbellies and rose in clumps from between their webbed toes as they writhed and complained.

From an obscure pocket beneath her shawl, the brunette removed a slender glass vial and a box of matches. She unstoppered the vial and shook a clear liquid over the cage, splashing it atop the horrors within. As the wind again blew toward them, Hawley recognized the stench of lantern oil. With a sharp strike of match against the side of the matchbox, a flame blossomed with a snap and a hiss, and she flung that, too, atop the cage.

The oil ignited instantly, and with a gasp of air, the flames quickly caught against the creatures' slime-shiny skin. Their screaming was drowned beneath the crackle of popping fat and blistering skin as they were cooked alive, their small bodies wreathed in a growing cloak of fire. The stench of their burning skin was tarry, tinged with ocean salt, and the crispy acridness of their black blood boiled and scorched.

Eventually, the frogmen went still as the fire feasted upon their remains. The woman had watched intently as they succumbed to the flames, and when the creatures finally fell silent, she turned sharply on a heel and walked with purpose through the crowd, back toward where she had come. Bystanders smartly stepped away, parting before her as if she were Moses, and slowly came back together in her wake, whispering nervously among themselves.

Hawley bent an ear toward the chattering, catching errant strands of overlapping conversations.

"Damnable witch, that one," an older man confided in his young partner. "Probably she brought those wretched things to shore."

Curious, Hawley finally put his back to the pyre and prodded his way through the slowly dissolving crowd to return to the tavern. He saw no sign of the woman until he was halfway up the stairs leading to his rented room, when something small and hard pressed into his lower back.

"Do not turn around," she said. "Open your door and enter your room. Raise your hands and keep your back to me until I say otherwise."

He nodded and, silently, did as instructed. The door groaned open, and he stepped inside, stopping in the center of the room, hands raised to his sides.

"I'm armed," he said.

"So am I."

Hawley couldn't help but smile. He nodded, keeping one ear cocked toward her as best he could.

"Turn around. Sit on the bed. Keep your hands where I can see them."

Again, he did as he was told and pressed his hands flat against the mattress.

"You keep interesting company." She waved the flintlock at Aldous's corpse. A trio of flies buzzed around his cratered face.

Hawley kept his eyes on the woman and his mouth shut.

"I haven't seen you here before," she said after a moment.

"Nor I, you, Miss…?"

"Those things." She nodded toward the door and the general area beyond, clearly meaning the caged creatures smoldering outside. "You brought them here."

Hawley shook his head. "No. I woke to the excitement they brought, though, and thought it best to see what was the fuss."

She nudged the flintlock a bit, exaggerating her aim toward Hawley's face. "It would be best if you do not lie."

Hawley's fingers clutched the edge of the mattress, his teeth gritting together. He detested having false accusations lobbed his way nearly as much as having a gun pointed toward his skull. "What were they?"

"You tell me."

"I swear, miss, I do not know. I suspect, though…" He drew in a deep breath, half-wondering if he were really, truly about to admit such a crazed notion. Crazed, yes, perhaps, but true enough nonetheless.

She eyed him suspiciously, waiting him out.

"I suspect they were not of this world. And I suspect they were summoned here by forces darker than either you or I could fathom."

Her hard, brown eyes continued to bore into his for a long, heart-stopping moment. Hawley was quite conscious of her finger on the trigger and the deep black bore of the pistol's barrel centered upon his forehead. Silently, she studied him, to the point that he very nearly felt her rooting around within his soul. And then the flintlock lowered.

Hawley's grip on the mattress loosened, and he exhaled loudly and with much relief. The muscles bunched in his shoulders relaxed slightly. Still, she continued to regard him, her eyes prompting him to continue.

"There is a book of magic and ancient lore," he said finally. "I haven't seen it myself, but I bore witness to the havoc it can wreak."

"Do tell," she said.

Hawley spoke slowly, a cold sweat breaking out upon his forehead and the nape of his neck. In the telling of his story, he relived the awful events of the New York Hospital. He spoke of various monstrosities: creatures both like and unlike anything he had seen previously; creatures very nearly like spiders, but not; creatures that ate flesh and bore their way into the bodies of their victims, to birth a thousand more of their numbers; and the massive, shelled beast with pointed limbs that had gored him and hoisted him off his feet. He barely noticed as his own hand moved of its own volition, his arm pressing against his belly to hug his wound.

"And somehow, you survived," she said.

"Myself and a number of others, and only just. We fought with fire and guns, and anything else we could. I very nearly died—would have, if not for my friend who dragged me away from the fray. The fighting lasted for days, the entire city consumed by violence, while I convalesced."

The woman seemed to consider his words, her hands now empty and the pistol secreted away somewhere on her person. He hadn't even noticed her pocket the weapon, so subtle and fluid had her movements been.

"Show me your wound."

"Ma'am?"

"Just show me," she said.

Nervously, Hawley unbuttoned his shirt, his eyes flitting between her and the door. He worried Post would intrude. If he, a black man, were caught alone with a white woman, in a state of undress, it would likely be the end of him. She at least had the sense to keep her distance as he unraveled the gauze. He shifted his hips atop the bed to better show her the injury.

"Good lord," she said.

He watched her eyes. For the first time, the hardness there softened into something more akin to fear. A large black circular scab was situated just above the curve of his belly, the flesh around it enflamed and empurpled. Pus slowly leaked a trail down his stomach, a network of red veins and traceries of black lines stretching across his flank.

After but a few strides, she was kneeling before him, her hands situated around the wound. Her thumbs and index fingers were aligned to create a triangle, the seeping injury in the center of this configuration like a bleeding eye. She began to speak words foreign and incongruous to Hawley's ears, her eyes shut, head tilted back. Her warm hands grew hotter against his skin, the weight of her body pressing harshly against him as her fingers began to pull open the flesh around his stitches. He grabbed at her wrists, intent on pushing her away, but the pain had sapped him of his strength almost immediately. Sweat exploded across his forehead as a sudden wave of nausea erupted in his belly. His arms shook, his legs weak and useless. The scabs buckled and broke. Yellow fluid poured out, turning to a noxious-smelling black. Even as he tried to pull away, she pushed closer. He tried to scream, but his voice was mysteriously absent. The pain grew more awful as her fingers gored him. She made a deadly triangular-shaped dagger of her hand, sinking her digits into him up to the third knuckle. Black and purple starbursts danced across his vision, his teeth clenched against the agony of her rooting around his innards, shifting and pulling at things inside him. Queasiness and a lightheadedness overtook him as the room around him swam in and out view. As his vision faded, he saw her pull back a web of blackened, slimy entrails. Their tendrils whipped uselessly about her wrist and forearm, struggling between her pinched fingers for escape. He sank back then saw nothing but the purest black as his eyelids slammed shut and his consciousness fled.

He woke moments later with little recollection of having passed out. His head ached with a vicious throbbing.

"Drink this." The woman held a glass of water toward him. She looked pale, and dark rings circled her tired eyes.

He sat up to take the glass, noticing only after he was erect that his belly did not protest the movement. There was no pain in his abdomen. His eyes lingered on the smooth expanse of skin as his mind struggled to process the vision. His injury was absent; the bruising that had surrounded it had faded to a yellowish ring. His stomach was still wet with fresh blood and pus, but the hole and the stitches that had bound it shut were inexplicably gone.

Her hands and arms were damp, but with water rather than gore. The water in the washbasin was brackish. A stained damp towel lay bunched on the table beside it.

"How?"

"You were dying, shrouded in a blanket of black magic that was growing ever tighter to strangle you to death. That was not merely a stab wound, you see, but a site of infestation."

"What did you do with it?" He looked beyond her for the creature that had taken up residence in his belly, but saw no sign of it.

"It is disposed of," she said. "Banished."

"Banished to where?"

"To where it came from."

He nodded and sipped slowly at the cup of blessedly clear, clean water. He thought of the cost such an esoteric practice might incur and decided she had gotten off lightly. She looked only somewhat sickly, but more exhausted than anything. Despite this, he recognized, too, an indefatigable spirit within her, one that was as hard as stone. Witch or not, she was strong.

"Your friend here," she said, delicately toeing the corpse, "he reeks of a curse. How did he die?"

"An accident, last night in the rain. A trunk struck him."

"I assure you, it was no accident."

"You're a witch, then?"

"I believe we share a common interest. I, too, am searching for *Al Azif,* and if what came out from the fisherman's catch today is any indication, we may both be already much too late."

"You didn't answer my question," Hawley said. "And what is your interest with this grimoire?"

"Call me what you like. A witch, a sorceress, a practitioner—it makes no difference. I am a Sister of Eibon, and our order seeks merely knowledge. We wish to possess *Al Azif* and protect it from misuse. I fear that, already, it has been much misused."

"Those things outside. You are familiar with such ghastliness, I presume?"

The brunette nodded, and it only now occurred to Hawley that he knew not even her name, nor did she know his.

"They were the offspring of Dagon, no doubt summoned here by the Esoteric Order—"

"Esoteric Order?"

"Cultists. There have been rumors of abductions, of missing children, urchins mostly. Dagon's worshippers sacrifice their victims to this dark god, calling forth its children to feast in exchange for riches and immortality. His children—the Deep Ones, as they are known—have been spreading across this land like a plague. First Innsmouth, to the north, and now here in Arkham. My sisters have encountered them in other small coastal villages between these two points, but for whatever reason, their concentration has grown strongest here."

Hawley ran a hand over his head, his brain protesting loudly that this was insane, nonsensical foolishness. The woman was mad or hysterical. Her claims were nothing more than rantings fit for the asylum.

But he could not dispel her accounts so easily, no matter how much the rational portions of his mind objected. He had seen the things in New York and heard the whispers of disappearances floating throughout the city. On the eve of the riots, his female acquaintance had told him of her fellow working girls who had disappeared, only for their remains to be found mutilated and with organs missing. Murder and magic had already coalesced into the summoning of arcane horrors. No, discounting her words was not merely a disservice, but an impossibility. Further, to regard her words as little more than crazed rantings was to deny what he had seen with his own eyes mere moments ago.

Oh, if only I could so easily discount such abominations, he thought ruefully. *If only it were so simple.*

He recalled rumors about Innsmouth, as well. The small town had earned some fame as a shipbuilding yard during the Revolution. There had been whispers about the town, the richness of its fishing industry, and the skill of its ship makers. But stranger claims had been made, as well, about the odd state of disrepair and rot that attacked the town like a pox. Hawley had heard remarks about the odd appearances of the folk who lived there and speculations about the uncanny losses in Continental Navy vessels originating from those particular shipyards. Rumors spoke of shipwrecks with few survivors and frigates that had been lost altogether. Not simply captured or destroyed, they had actually *vanished* at sea, their crew never to be seen or heard from again. At the time, he had considered these stories to be little more than campfire tales told by weary soldiers. Now, though, he wondered.

"I've not heard of this Dagon before," he said.

"He is one of the ancients, an elder god of fish and fertility. His offspring require human mates in order to survive, and they conspire with the Esoteric Order to breed. Much of Arkham's fishing ventures are successful, largely because of this compact. And so when the urchins go missing, everybody is more than happy to look the other way."

"Those… *things*… then, they were human?"

"Partly so, but I would not attribute to them many human qualities at all. They are monsters through and through."

"And this order, what do they want with the book *Al Azif?*"

"To raise Dagon to his complete glory," she said. "To make him not just the god of seas but king of this realm and ruler of the Earth itself."

Hawley stood, only partly surprised that the woman made no attempt to step away. She stood her ground, and although she looked wary, there was not so much a trace of fear about her. She trusted him, for whatever reason, as evidenced by her confiding in him. But was she looking for an ally, or perhaps an accomplice, or something worse? He knew not and found he was not nearly as troubled as he perhaps should have been. Although she had held him at gunpoint, she had also healed him. There existed between them an openness, and he felt he could trust her as well.

Or perhaps she's merely bewitched me, he mused idly. For as strange as this town clearly was, this Sister of Eibon felt oddly normal, and given all that life had seen fit to bring Salem Hawley's way, he felt due some measure of normalcy, regardless of how small.

"We are looking for a woman," he said, pacing the small room. In only a matter of steps, he had reached the opposite wall and was forced to turn back toward the bed. "A Dr. Heather Ellery. She absconded from New York with *Al Azif* and returned with it here, to her hometown."

"Ellery. Damnit, I should have known." Her fingers curled into tight fists, and she was clearly waging war to relax her body. "But… You are sure? There has been no sightings of Ellery in quite some time."

"After the commotion in New York, several of the town's doctors were believed to have fled. But, later, their bodies were discovered. Or at least some of them were. Two remain unaccounted for, one of whom was born in Manhattan. The other, Ellery, disappeared entirely and was thought to have returned here."

"And how did you learn of this?" the woman asked.

"What is your name, miss? Mine is Salem. Salem Hawley."

A roguish smile crossed her lips as she extended her hand. "Salem, eh? That's most curious. Perhaps our meeting was even more fortuitous than I had imagined. I am Louise LéMarche."

"Louise." He took her hand and placed a brief, gentle kiss upon her middle knuckle. "I owe a debt to one Dr. Richard Bayley, who treated me in the aftermath of the city's riots. He seeks this book, as well, to destroy it. I am to square my account with him by recovering the tome and returning with it to the city."

She nodded then mused, "Destroying *Al Azif* may perhaps be the best option, given its capacity for misuse by mankind."

Hawley returned to the bed and sat, cupping his hands between his knees. "I believe that may be the most suitable course of action. Given the fate of poor Aldous, I suspect returning the book to New York might only create more problems."

Louise nodded, waiting for Hawley to explain further.

"You say Aldous was cursed, and I suspected it briefly, before dismissing it as too improbable. But that was foolish of me. He *was* cursed, and by his employer and the son-in-law of Dr. Bayley, no less. I see now that I fell for Bayley's ruse too easily, and under the hand of his and Post's drugging, I was blinded."

"Then your life, too, is yet in danger."

"Yes, well, such is the case always in this young nation of ours."

He meant the words to be light and self-depreciating, but Louise's eyes turned downcast, as if he'd struck a chord. She appeared ready to speak then thought better of it.

"We must end this meeting for now, miss," Hawley said, sparing her any further embarrassment. "I'm to take Dr. Post to the university, and I suspect it would be wise to not raise his suspicions of me more than they may be already."

She nodded again, looking, for the first time, quite demure. "Safe travels, Mr. Hawley. We shall meet again."

"I've no doubt," he said.

Louise opened the door but a minor crack, enough to peer into the hallway and see toward the stairs beyond. Judging it empty, she stepped out and closed the door behind her. Hawley listened for a moment to the sound of her footfalls receding down the corridor and to the steps below.

Haunted by the anguish of dying frogmen and the sight of Aldous's head caving in beneath the weighted corner of Post's trunk, he felt for the gun at his side and the blade at his waist, seeking some measure of reassurance. Then he bent to lift Aldous over his shoulder and escort the body to the carriage below. There was much work left to do, and the day was yet early.

Chapter 9

HAWLEY SAT HUNCHED AGAINST the storm, the horse's reins clutched in his frozen fingers. A soaked blanket was wrapped around his shoulders, for what little good it did him. The chill was bone-deep, the rain unrelenting. Almost immediately upon Hawley and Post's leaving the inn, the skies had turned frightfully dark with black clouds, and frigid winds assailed them. Lightning shot through the sky, following by a deafening boom of thunder. Above him, on the rooftop cargo hold, lay Aldous, a quiet companion whose head was cocked at a severe and unnatural angle, his clothes equally soaked through and pasted to his frail frame.

Rain poured from the heavens, obliterating Hawley's sight and whatever lay ahead. He could barely see past the swaying hips of the horses directly in front of him. As the carriage cut a path through Arkham proper, he caught the rare sight of black-clad, human-sized shapes hidden beneath parasols flitting through the city square. Life within the town appeared to have returned to normalcy in the wake of those creatures' mysterious appearance and their prompt demise at the hands of Louise LéMarche.

Or at least as normal as Arkham could be presumed to be, he thought somewhat bitterly. The whole town seemed to be situated at all times amid either an unending downpour or beneath a thick blanket of fog. What little he had seen of Arkham had been, thus far, duly unimpressive. The buildings were constantly slick with moisture, the gaps between bricks green with moss, and wooden trim swollen and waterlogged. Even the floors of the lodge had begun to warp and buckle and were perpetually soft underfoot. Where walls met the floor there was evidence of black mold, and around the doorframe of his rented room, the threshold and trim had taken on a dark, chewed-upon look of slow decay.

Flashes of lightning revealed just how distraught the town was, and Hawley couldn't help but think again of all he had heard about the foulness of Innsmouth. Arkham, it seemed, suffered from similar degradations. Even in the days leading to their approach of the town itself, Hawley had felt preternaturally damp and cold, to boot. The smell of wood rot, wet earth, and vegetation had been as omnipresent as the mud at their feet or churned beneath the horse's hooves and the carriage's wheels. If he had but one word to describe Arkham and his own disposition within the town, it would be *sodden.* Given Aldous's fate, however, Hawley was happy to take damp and cold over cursed and dead, even if his mood was unnaturally soured as a result.

The horses lumbered through the muck, slogging slowly through the trail to Miskatonic University. With each step the horses took, mud squelched and sprayed beneath their metal shoes. Although the distance was not great, the severity of the road and the weather made it more than a miserable hour's travel. From his bench, Hawley spotted the occasional hopping shape along the side of the woods. Thinking of those damnable frogmen and their death cries sent an icy shiver through him, and he wondered if what leapt in the shadows beyond the tree line was even natural or another of those ungodly abominations.

The air stank of rotting leaves and lightning-scorched sky, and Mother Nature gave no indication that she would be finished raining the unrelenting piss upon them anytime soon. To be sure, the only bright side was that Miskatonic drew near, and with another rapid-fire crack of lightning, the campus was briefly illuminated beyond the gates encircling the wide stretch of property, which appeared deserted.

As the stagecoach drew nearer, Hawley saw that the gate had been opened for them. He saw no sign of guardsmen, doormen, or gatekeepers, though. Post had sent a missive to the university notifying them of his arrival, and clearly it had been paid some heed, even if everyone appeared to be hiding from the foul weather. At the least, it prevented Hawley from having to stop the carriage and fuss with the entry himself, and for that, he was grateful. The horses continued on, following the wide muddy trail to the center building, the largest fixture of the campus. Although a number of windows were illuminated from the interior by candlelight, Hawley saw no sign of students, faculty, or administrators on the campus grounds, no doubt due to the savage weather. Not until the horses drew the stagecoach alongside the main building did he see a bustle of movement as the main entryway burst open with a flurry of motion and the unsnapping of umbrellas for Dr. Post to step beneath as he ejected himself from the carriage.

"Dr. Post," one man said, shouting to be heard over the rain pounding against his parasol as he extended a hand in greeting, "I am Dr. Heinrich Kohl, and this"—he motioned toward the tall, rail-thin man beside him—"is Dr. Patrick Ellery."

Kohl spoke with a thick German accent, and much of his face was hidden by a patchy gray beard and unkempt mustache. His gray suit was equally unkempt, although his blue eyes were studiously pointed. He waved for a trio of students to come forth, leading Post away from the carriage.

Hawley unfolded his numb limbs from the bench, willing his knees to cooperate as he stepped down. One student was already on the step, astride the carriage, reaching up to grab hold of Aldous. They cared not a whit for the man's handling, and the student yanked viciously on Aldous's arm, quite nearly tearing off the man's shirtsleeve, and sent the body toppling off the coach's roof. The body struck the mud with an unceremonious splat, landing facedown, to the delight of the three youths. There, two of them took possession of the body, one on each end, while the third led the way toward the anatomists' lecture hall, gleefully shouting commands. They ran with the corpse, heads bowed, into the wind and lashing rains, their laughter drowned by the storm.

Hawley's fists curled at his side at the injustice of it all, but especially at the disgusting joy the young students displayed at Aldous's mortal remains. Only weeks prior, Hawley had waged a war of words in the *New York Daily Advertiser* against the resurrectionists plaguing the Black cemetery in Manhattan. The war had culminated in a city-wide riot against the medical professionals responsible for the scores of grave robberies. So very little had changed, despite his best efforts, and his temper flared at the ignominy of it all. He also realized how little he knew about Aldous. Did the man have a family or any loved ones who would be concerned about his passing and who were now being denied their right to bury him properly? Hawley fought to keep his composure, even as his incense at Post and the whole of this university rose. He wanted to club those children over the head, return Aldous home, and pay his respects to whomever the man left behind. Instead, he stood quietly, letting the cold rain tamp down his burning anger.

"I am sorry for your loss," Kohl said to Post. His eyes flicked over Hawley with an instant dismissal before returning his full attention to a fellow man of science. "But, as you know, he will serve mankind in a grander purpose in death than he ever would have in life."

"To God's ear," Post said, bowing his head in acknowledgement.

"Come, come. Let us escape this dreariness and enjoy our lunch!"

Hawley made to follow, but Post stopped him immediately, pressing a hand against Salem's chest. "You, of course, will wait here for my return." Post gave a shove, and Hawley stepped back, biting his tongue as he was so often forced to in the doctor's company.

Kohl led his companions inside, the ornately carved and darkly stained oak doors closing behind them. Hawley gave the other men a moment to move deeper inside the building, letting the rainfall wash over him. Despite the cold wind and fury of the storm, he would not be waiting inside the stagecoach carriage for Post's return. Instead, he circled to the side of the building and, through the impressive gilded windows, watched their progress, following along from the outside.

Thanks to the copper wall lanterns illuminating the interior of the hall, he could easily see the men inside. Rainwater streaked the windowpanes as the men talked affably, giving them the appearance of an oil painting reduced to streaked shapes. At one point, Ellery clapped Post on the back, and Kohl said something that made the trio laugh.

Miskatonic's grounds were well-kept, and as Hawley crept along the wall, he searched for students or other signs of life outside. He saw no one and felt confident the weather would keep him largely obscured from the eyes of others, as well, unless somebody approached the opposite side of the window and looked directly upon his pathetically sodden form. A number of trees separated the campus's various buildings such that each was an island all its own. This administration building was especially secluded among dense stands of cedar, and well-hidden on three of its four sides.

The men passed through a massive entry and into a spacious dining room intimately lit by a number of chandeliers. Kohl was still speaking, and Post's posture indicated he was listening intently. The group moved to a table situated away from the other diners, no doubt to afford them some measure of privacy, but also away from the windows. There would be no way for Hawley to hear them, nor even to attempt reading their lips.

He crouched beside the window, nestled in a small gap between hydrangea bushes ringing the building at regular intervals, simply to observe for a time. The dining room was sparsely populated, but those present were finely dressed, all male, and clustered in groups of two or three. He suspected they were faculty members, and a dozen or so servants attended them, bringing water or ale and various dishes of food, desserts, and port.

What caught his eye, though, were the tall pillars situated at regular intervals against the walls. The items atop each pillar were encased in glass. Inside the cases were skulls of various shapes and sizes, some almost canine like. Others seemed borderline human but were clearly not. These latter were either much too large or featured oddities such as large, ridged brows, narrow orbital cavities, and teeth that were obscenely inhuman. One skull featured spiraling horns, like a goat's. Knife-like protuberances jutted forth along either side of the mouth of another. Staring at any of them for a length of time was enough to disturb him greatly, and he forced his eyes to break away, again surveying the woods at the property's perimeter.

From within the thick forestry, he saw no signs of movement. He did, however, smell something awfully pungent that resembled the stink of rotting fish. Recalling the map of the area he had seen prior to leaving New York, he knew the Miskatonic River cut a trail beyond the borders of the university as it wound its way toward Kingsport and the Atlantic Ocean beyond. Within the woods, too, were a number of ponds, such as Beck Pond, the closest.

Moreover, although the smell carried a foul, salty fish smell, it reminded him of an odor he had scented fairly recently—that very morning, in fact—and was not likely to soon forget. It had not escaped him that Dr. Ellery was among Post's company, and Hawley found it an unlikely coincidence that the man should share the same surname as Dr. Heather Ellery, the cultist who had stolen *Al Azif*. The stink he recognized all too well as belonging to those frogmen abominations, and to be but on the other side of the wall from a man he now believed to be a member of the Esoteric Order of Dagon alongside his bride was simply too much to be random happenstance.

Keeping his form hunched beneath the window, Hawley hurried across the clearing and dashed into the woods. The smell was even more noxious there, and it instantly made him lightheaded and nauseated. As he pushed past the tree line and headed deeper into the woods, he began to breathe through his mouth, pressing the back of his hand against his nostrils. It was no use, though, and he could practically taste the heady fumes. Drawing nearer the river, the toxic stench grew all the more repugnant, carried directly to him on a strong, hard, ill wind.

Rain slamming against the leafy canopy and the roiling boom of thunder made it difficult to discern, but he believed he heard, briefly, a long, suffering wail of agony. Immediately, he pressed himself against the trunk of the nearest tree. He searched the vicinity from around the thick trunk, but saw nothing. He strained to hear and only barely caught the noises of pained grunting. Whoever, or whatever, was making such strange and strangled noises was close, but still out of sight. Crouched low yet again, he dashed ahead, fleet of foot and as silent as was possible. He paused at the next tree, scanning the land around him, then moved onto the next trunk and the next. In this fashion, he drew closer; the grunting and wailing growing louder.

Even through the rain, he could hear the angry currents of the Miskatonic and see that the river rode high in its banks. Not much longer and with just a bit more rain, it would flood the valley. He made this observation in spite, or perhaps in defiance, of what his eyes saw immediately before him. The simple truth was he mentally *refused* to see what was plainly before him. He could only deny what his eyes reported for so long, though, and their movements drew and demanded his full attention.

Three human-sized creatures squatted before him in the woods, well enough away from the river banks and the potential flood zones. Although their forms approximated those of human beings, they were plainly otherwise. Their flesh was the pale white of fish bellies, their faces a distressing mix of human and amphibian, and it occurred to his shocked mind that these were the adult equivalent of the creatures LeMarché had torched earlier in the day.

All women, they were nude. Their breasts were flaccid sacs tipped by long, rope-like nipples. Their hands were caked in mud from the holes they had dug and were squatting over. Each held onto her own knees, gripping so tightly that her knuckles were even whiter than her body, legs spread over either side of the shallow pit.

For a moment, Hawley thought they were urinating. He watched with both disgust and a certain entrancement that came from having stumbled upon a scene he had no business witnessing yet felt compelled to observe. After a moment, he realized that the stream issuing from each woman's sex was something wholly other than piss. He squinted against the rain, watching as one frog woman reached between her legs, her fingers curling through the soaked and matted hair that covered her labia, to gather the tiny, spherical, orange flecks that had clung to the curls of pubic hair. She shook her fingers over the small trench, depositing the tiny beads among the bed of others. She stayed squatting there for a moment, her teeth clenched. Then her gut roiled with a spasm, and she let forth a choked scream.

Hawley felt fouled deeply in his soul from bearing witness to the unnatural display, but his eyes refused to break away. A dozen score more of those orange jewels were flushed from the creature's body, and although he could not hear them, he imagined the sounds of their clinking against one another as the eggs jostled for space. The women were breathing raggedly, clearly spent and exhausted. They stood, legs quivering, and pushed the mud back into place over the clutches of eggs they had laid.

Hand in hand, they joined in a circle and embraced. The gills on either side of their necks fluttered. Their oversized, pitch-black eyes blinked as their faces appeared to soften. They trilled softly to one another as they held one another close, squeezing hands. Finally, they slowly broke away. One by one, they stepped into the river and sank beneath its churning, dark depths, disappearing from view.

Hawley's heart beat rapidly, and he gasped suddenly, unaware that he had ceased breathing. His lungs ached fiercely from deprivation. His mind swirled with dark intent. Half-nauseous and half-incensed, he stepped from around the tree and strode toward the nearest nest, which was already so heavily pounded by rain that it was nearly impossible to detect where the earth had once been disturbed. He was overcome with horror and the sudden urge to destroy. He planned on unburying the eggs and stomping them out of existence.

"Shame you had to see that," a low voice said.

Startled, Hawley turned toward the speaker and saw behind him a trio of men. He recognized them as the students who had carted Aldous into the medical school. When he had seen them earlier, the thick downpour had made their features indistinct and murky, revealing only the general forms of their bodies. They were closer now than they had been previously, and this near, he could see their deformities.

Each had a slightly misshapen face. The shelves of their foreheads protruded over their eyes farther than any normal man's. Their lips, thin and colorless, pursed of their own accord. Their eyes were much too big, much too round, and bulged unnaturally from their sockets. Their ears were small and set low on either side of their heads, quite nearer to their necks. With only the slightest hint of a bridge, their olfactory organ was little more than a pair of sunken hollows. Although their faces were more spherical than they should have been atop such thick, stunted necks, the absence of features gave each man a queer flatness.

Shocked into stillness, Hawley could do little more than assess his options as the men spread out around him. The speaker, the largest of the three, and his thick, barrel-chested companion strode forward. With the other man flanking him and moving slightly behind him, Hawley had little recourse, and their intent was plain.

His hand, as fast as a snake, darted beneath his coat and latched upon the grip of his flintlock. Even still, he realized, he was far too late. Time moved slowly. The world itself paused in horror at the display that revealed itself. The man standing before him opened his mouth, his jaw seeming to unhinge, and his tongue leapt forth from between teeth that looked more at home within a bear trap than in any human mouth.

Hawley was too slow—too human—to escape the impossibly long and narrow muscle that lashed toward him and struck him in the throat. A sharp smack of flesh on flesh and a painful sting left Hawley senseless, and he collapsed to his knees. The pain was immediate, an electric fire twisting through his skull, and breathing was impossible. The passage in his throat had narrowed, leaving him gasping for air as he writhed in the mud.

The very last thing he saw were the trio of men tightening their circle around him. Two men hoisted him up, folding his arms around their shoulders, leaving his feet to drag through the soaked earth. And then the world itself disappeared, folding in upon itself in the darkness, with only a painful wheeze to note its sudden absence.

Chapter 5

S LOWLY, SALEM HAWLEY CAME to, his eyes opening to the darkness. Several moments passed before his vision adjusted to the dim candlelight. He was in a large laboratory separated from the working area by a barred jail-cell door. Hawley had been left to recover on a cold stone floor, and his body ached as he shifted and stood. His muscles felt strained, and they protested with each of his movements. Swallowing, he winced against the pain in his dry throat. The muscles there threatened to seize as though he had been only recently choked. It occurred to him, too, that he had no idea how long he had been out.

"Your aches are from a paralytic agent," a woman's voice said, "secreted by our salivary glands."

He caught a flutter of movement beyond his cage, and he peered harder into the dimly lit chamber beyond. The speaker aided his search by stepping more fully into the light, an action that brought her nearly a finger's breadth away. Surprised, Hawley stepped back in reflex, expecting another attack, but also shocked and repulsed by the woman's appearance.

"How will I know her?" he'd asked Dr. Bayley shortly after being pressed into the man's service.

"Her features," Bayley had said, "are quite distinguishable. Such that, I suspect, you will have no trouble identifying her at all."

And so it was. Nude, Dr. Heather Ellery stood before him, her appearance unlike that of any other woman he had ever witnessed. She was plainly inhuman, but unlike the frogwomen he had witnessed laying their eggs on the shores of the Miskatonic. No, this woman, indeed, was cut from another rib.

She was tall and thin, her spine straight and shoulders squared, bearing a proud and commanding demeanor that was inescapable. Her eyes were overlarge black spheres set at forty-five-degree angles on either side of her flat nostrils, her mouth small and churlish. Rather than a full head of hair, her scalp was studded with spiky bristles like that of a stinging nettle. Similar barbed hairs stood along her bare arms and legs, and cut a trail from her pubis to sternum. Her skin was a pale, honeydew green, but around the spiky hairs and encircling her eyes, the flesh was a pronounced dark maroon. A strange, mucus-like slickness covered her body, casting a wet sheen over her flesh. Reflected candlelight danced upon her as she drew closer so that she practically glowed in the orange light.

"Where am I?" Hawley asked, his voice raspy as he dredged the words from the barrel of his throat.

A slight breeze whispered past his neck, incensing the hairs there to stand on end. The brickwork was a darker shade of red than normal, having absorbed the room's dampness. A steady trickle of moisture followed the tracery of masonry to join the small standing puddle in one corner, where the cell's floor sloped downward.

"You are still on university grounds," Ellery said. Her voice was as fluid as her body. The harmony of her words was entirely discordant with her physical form. She sounded so utterly human, to the point of banality, or so it should have been if her visage were not so revolting. She walked slowly past his cell, her fingers trailing against the bars of his cell doors and leaving behind a thin, shimmering film. "In the basement of the medical school. During the war, several captured redcoats were housed here. This lab itself had been modified into a makeshift prison, an aesthetic that has proved useful despite the war's resolution."

His eyes still adjusting to the gloom, Hawley was able to make out another three cells opposite him. He judged himself to be in the middle cell of another three on his side of the laboratory. Across the way, several pairs of eyes found his. Children's eyes. He recalled LeMarché's mention of missing urchins. He had, perhaps, discovered those abducted souls.

In the center of the room, though, leather straps affixing him to a dissection table, was Dr. Wright Post. The doctor was unconscious, and a trio of husky, stooped men loomed over him. Hawley had little trouble recognizing them. A knot of muscles threatened to seize in his throat at the sight of them. Hawley's eyes roamed the room, skirting around the edges of Ellery's form, doing all he could to avoid meeting her gaze.

She stepped close to the cell door, so that she filled the entirety of his sight. "If you are looking for *Al Azif*, you will not find it here. And don't look so surprised. Of course I know why you are here."

Her words shook Hawley to the core. His eyes flittered back to Post, beyond the creature's shoulder. Internally, he cursed Post, mentally raging against the confined betrayer. "And now you shall kill us both. Is that it?"

Ellery barked loose the most awful and grating laugh Salem Hawley had ever heard. The noise was akin to glass breaking in a hailstorm. "No. No, not yet, anyway. The both of you can serve us yet. It is why Dr. Bayley sent you here, after all."

Hawley's mouth fell open, the simple word dying on his lips, even as his mind attempted to calculate the meaning of her words. *Bayley?*

The woman turned her back to the captive and strode to the dissection table. She got a knee up over the edge and hoisted herself atop the table, crawling atop Post. Hawley attempted to avert his eyes, but his will and curiosity contested against more primal and insidious desires. His damnable eyes followed the curve of her shifting rump, to the narrow lips of her exposed and glistening sex, as she worked her way from the foot of the table to its head. Her knees came to rest on either side of Post's face, then the bristling hairs surrounding the core of her womanhood stood erect, brushing the doctor's lips as her hips moved in slow circles. Post's mouth opened of its own accord. He twitched, attempting to move his head away from the tickling hairs, but his skull was constrained by a thick leather strap pinning him in place.

Despite his revulsion, Hawley found himself enraptured by the display. He had to swallow back the scream that burned in his gut as his mind flashed back to the scene he had witnessed immediately prior to his capture. His mind rallied against the horror of Ellery's intent as her fingers reached between Post's lips and the lips of her sex. Hawley watched helplessly as fluid dribbled into Post's mouth.

The unconscious doctor's tongue licked the discharge from his lips, his face crinkling in distaste. He did not rouse, though, and Hawley surmised that whatever paralytic agent had been used on him must have been similarly applied to Post.

Ellery reached down to pry apart Post's jaw. A rush of tiny orange beads ejected from between her legs and poured into his widely opened mouth. What seemed like dozens upon dozens of small amber eggs flooded past his lips before the flow halted. The men surrounding the table moved quickly. One slammed Post's jaw shut, while another clamped his nose, forcing the man to swallow what he'd been fed. With his breathing cut off, Post's eyes flared open in shock. His body reared up against the restraints at what must have been fright over the sight before him. The men forced him to lie still against the table, and as Ellery moved off the table, Hawley could see all too well the workings of Post's throat as he swallowed. His face was screwed up in apparent distaste and horror. When he was finally released, his mouth opened, and he drew in great, gasping breaths, his face red. Post then began coughing, perhaps attempting to vomit up his recent meal, but to no avail.

"What did you do to me?" Post shouted, over and over. He found Ellery, screaming, "What did you do?"

She merely smiled, her face transformed into malevolence chilling enough to silence him at last.

The odd men gave him a moment to collect himself before two of them began to unstrap him from the table and helped him off. The third led Post to a cell door then sealed the doctor inside.

"This is all your fault, you stupid pickaninny bastard," Post said, glaring harshly at Hawley.

Salem said nothing, but he did make a vow in that moment. In the darkest chamber of his most secret heart, Salem Hawley made himself a promise to kill Dr. Wright Post before all this was over. If he, himself, lived long enough, that was.

The muscled breeds of half-human, half-frog monstrosities lumbered toward his cell door. The leader produced a key to open it, and his two companions stepped inside. Hawley knew fighting was useless at that very moment, such that he did not even step back from the creatures. He would bide his time and fight at the appropriate hour, but at that moment, he could do little aside from brave it. This country, he knew, was no home for cowards, and it did not brook weakness well.

One muscled brute stepped forward, slamming a club-like fist into Hawley's middle. Although he had prepared himself for the punch, the hardness with which it was delivered still surprised him and stole the air from his lungs. He doubled over as meaty hands encircled his arms, hauling him forward. His feet left the floor as he was roughly manhandled onto the table. Thick leather straps were pulled tightly across his ankles, wrists, chest, and head to bind him. Movement was a sheer impossibility.

Ellery climbed atop the table, crawling toward him with black purpose. Her eyes found his and held them in her stare. He struggled uselessly against his bindings, but refused to break her glare. He stared into those deep pools of stygian darkness and did not blink.

As either side of her legs pressed around his waist, she reared up, straightening her torso as she kneed her way to the head of the table and situated herself over Hawley's face. Her fingers pushed through the bristly nettle of spiked hairs, her index and middle digits forming a V as they spread apart the labial lips hiding her sex. He saw all too clearly the pale fishbelly-white tissue surrounding the core of her birth canal. The small clutch of eggs was already breaching deep inside her, held together in gossamer, spiderweb-like strands of fluid.

"Open his mouth," Ellery demanded.

Thick fingers pressed painfully against either side of his face. His teeth sliced open his cheeks as his mouth was both squeezed and pried apart. A clear, viscous fluid ejected from her and splattered against his face. Stinking of rotten fish, it sluiced over his unwilling tongue, and he gagged on the briny taste.

Ellery pulled her sex wider, and the muscles lining her chasm flexed as she pushed the eggs forward on a wash of thick fluid. She lowered herself, pressing her genitals tightly to his mouth, and squeezed again.

Hawley felt sick to his stomach, overcome by both the rancid taste and awful stench. Her bristling hairs instantly irritated his skin, stabbing into his face and lips like needles. Another wash of briny fluid flushed across his tongue, then small, hard objects began to pelt the back of his throat. He choked on them, his stomach already revolting as he gagged on the rush of eggs flooding into his mouth. His throat worked involuntarily, half-choking upon and half-swallowing all he was given as quickly as he could, unable to resist despite his desperation.

Then the press of her organ against him and the knife points of her hairs were released, and she slid off him. Instantly, hands clamped against his mouth to seal his lips, while fingers pinched his nose shut, holding his skull in place. He was forced to swallow the entire final clutch of eggs, his stomach greasy with illness. As his throat finally relaxed, so too did the men's grip on his head, and he was allowed to breathe. He felt faint, queasy, and so very, very exposed.

The leather straps came undone and the men turned their backs to him as they plodded away. In a matter of moments, they were gone, but he could still hear their heavy footfalls against a nearby stairwell.

Hawley swallowed dryly, dazed and reeling. The appalling aftertaste of what had been done to him, what he had been forced to do, lingered in both his mouth and his mind, a dark churning of violation strumming throughout the entirety of his being. He moved quickly, leaning over the edge of the table in time for a gush of rotting fluid to rise out of him and splatter upon the floor. He gagged repeatedly, spitting out the reeking taste, but to no avail. His belly clenched and heaved, and another gout of clear, foul liquid ejected from his stomach. His mouth filled again with the taste of rotting fish. His innards were in a paroxysm of all-out rebellion, his throat clenching and unclenching as his stomach rumbled and pitched. Tears stung his eyes.

Despite all of the liquid he had thrown up, he still felt ungodly full, and he could feel the clumped shapes gathered painfully in his throat. When he looked down at the mess on the floor, he saw only watery remains. The eggs were still inside him. He clenched his eyes shut, mentally raging. *No, no, no!*

"They will only release on their own accord," Post said from behind him. His voice was thick and husky, and Hawley imagined the man's throat must feel as raw as his own. "And by then, it will be far too late."

Hawley turned on the table to meet the white man's gaze. Post was pale, his skin as white as a freshly woven bedsheet.

"No," Salem said, refusing to believe the man. "There must be a way. There has to be."

He flung his legs over the side of the autopsy table and shoved himself off. He strode immediately to the caged urchins and grabbed at their cell door, fully expecting to meet the resistance of a lock. He nearly fell back onto his ass in surprise, quite unprepared for the door to open at his first pull. Small, sad eyes met his. Where there should have been an imploring need for help, there was only defeat.

"Come with me," he said, holding a hand to one boy. The child looked at the black man's hand, ignored it, but pushed himself to his feet regardless. He spoke in a foreign tongue to his cellmates, a small knot of boys, a few young girls, all of them streaked in mud and gore. The closest boy, cheeks red and inflamed, had a swollen jaw, and small dots of blood stood out against the flesh where he'd been stabbed with pinprick hairs.

So, she's—his mind stumbled as he deliberately sought to avoid the word *impregnated*—*infected them, as well.*

Leading the boys out of the cell, he was stopped briefly by a hand jutting from its cage, reaching toward him. "Please, don't leave me. You can't leave me."

Hawley looked at Post then turned away. A hurried scrambling sounded as he passed, and Post shouted in a moment of panic, his hands gripping the bars of his cell door, shaking them hard. With a squeal of hinges, the cell door opened.

"It was… It was open?" Post asked, his surprise only partly amused. The question of *why* hung unspoken on his lips.

Hawley found the stairs in short order, but was unable to escape the disquiet surrounding him. The men had all but disappeared, and Ellery was nowhere to be seen. He took the stairs to the door at the top and was again surprised when it offered no resistance. The door opened to a darkened corridor devoid of people. An entrance was at either end of the long hallway, and a spectral flash of lightning revealed the tree line at the far end, placing the Miskatonic River at the building's rear. He knew better than to head that way and led the group toward the nearer entrance. As he approached the foyer, from the corner of his eye, a strange sight caught his attention, stopping him. On a bulletin board hung near the door, a collection of printed and handwritten flyers drew his eyes. Only one in particular was of note. He quickly snatched it off the board and hastily crumpled it into a pocket. He prayed for time later to study it properly, then he was shoving through the door.

The rain hit his skin in hard spikes, instantly irritating his bruised and chapped mouth as his face met the inclement weather. As it had been when they arrived, the small university appeared to be all but devoid of life. *Where is everybody?* he wondered. *Where did Ellery and her thugs run off to?*

The Miskatonic, most likely, he decided. Perhaps they needed to recharge, to moisten their skin after having been inside for so long. He gave it little thought, though, content merely in their absence. The fact of the matter was, he knew nothing of their biology or lifestyles. They could be anywhere, and so he led the group cautiously, but quickly, along the path leading back to the administrator's hall. As luck would have it, the horses and carriage were as they had been left, the animals soaked to the bone and clearly uneasy.

"You children ride in here," he said, opening the stagecoach door and helping the waterlogged urchins inside. When Post attempted to board, Hawley put a hand to the man's chest and pushed him back.

"You ride with me."

Post deflated almost instantly, although Hawley found little glee in the man's altered attitude. The doctor's defiance and haughtiness had clearly been curbed, if not completely tamed, by recent events. And although Hawley still wished the man ill, he could not also deny Post's newfound pitifulness.

"You owe me answers," Hawley rasped through his clogged throat once they were situated upon the driver's bench. The horses nimbly found their way back to the university's entrance and back onto the long stretch of road to Arkham proper.

"Bayley," Post said immediately. "Bayley betrayed me. He betrayed both of us."

"*Al Azif* was never stolen, was it?"

Post shook his head, his eyes locked onto some point off in the distance. His whole body shivered beneath his soaked clothes and the ice-cold rain. Hawley had been nearly convinced the man hadn't heard him and was about to repeat the question when Post finally answered.

"No," he said. "Bayley gave it to Ellery, told her to leave New York immediately and that I was to follow. When he saw what had been done to you, though, he thought it best to wait until you could travel."

"Why was I needed at all?" Hawley demanded, fuming.

Post looked at him with something akin to awe, and for the first time, there was no trace of hate. "You were touched by a god, and you lived. That is a rare thing, indeed. It also meant that your sacrifice would be that much more powerful."

Hawley's stomach lurched, unseating a foul, fish-tinged belch. He swallowed uncomfortably.

"After the situation in New York grew untenable, Ellery proposed an alternative. Bayley reluctantly agreed, but decided that the continuation of his work, even in the hands of another, was ultimately worth it. Bayley, you see, is loyal to a different god. Ellery, meanwhile, is an heir of Dagon, and she seeks to use *Al Azif* to restore his order on Earth and restore her people's standing as rulers of both land and sea. She and Bayley may be of differing factions, but their goals are ultimately the same, and thus, a truce was brokered."

Their goals, Hawley thought bitterly. *To destroy the human race and hand this world over to an ancient god they called Dagon.* "With me in the middle."

"The ignorant savage. A role you play well," Post said, with a small amount of mirth.

Hawley flushed with anger at the doctor's epithet, but he tamped it down. He couldn't very well stop in the middle of the trail and beat the man to death, as much as he would have liked. No, he needed to return to Arkham, to LeMarché.

"Why are they doing any of this? Why summon this Dagon here?"

"Why do you pray or attend Sunday mass? If you had the chance to meet your god, would you not seize it?"

Hawley wanted to argue, but words failed him. There was no discounting the madness of religious devotion or the fervor it could drive some men toward. At that very moment, on the opposite side of the Atlantic, the Spanish Inquisition was still underway after hundreds of years. Its death toll continued to rise as it claimed the lives of heretics, Muslims, and Jews, all in the foolhardy belief that empowering men of a particular faith through atrocity was in service to God himself. Logic and humane rationality could do little to win against violent insanity.

The carriage jostled behind Hawley as the wheels hit a rut and continued to jounce even as the earth leveled out. A loud crack sounded directly at his ear, catching his attention, although he knew not at all what was occurring inside the stagecoach.

"It's beginning," Post said, his voice both prideful and pained. He clutched his sodden coat tightly around his chest, his knuckles beneath his chin.

Hawley kept his focus on the path ahead, urging the horses forward through the fog and rain. The wooden wall of the carriage muffled the sudden screams of urchins inside.

Their exact words were lost to him under the storm, but the loud thud of a body slamming into the wall was noisome even in the downpour. The wood at his back heaved.

He pressed the horses on, worried that it was already much too late—both for the urchins and for himself, although he had yet to feel the ill effects of what had been forced upon him by Ellery.

As the cacophony in the carriage grew, he began to see a glimmer of light piercing the veil of fog ahead, and he knew he was close to Arkham. The trail had taken him across a bridge he recalled from his journey to the university, and now it followed the serpentine path of the Miskatonic River. Arkham itself was situated on either side of the river's banks, and the lanterns at the town's entrance were a minor beacon as he drew nearer.

A loud scream rang in his ear, and he hunched away from it instinctively, flicking the horse's reins and demanding they go faster. *Faster, damnit!*

Even with the rain and fog, the noises of revelry were loud. While he and Post had been otherwise occupied away from Arkham, the town's residents had been preparing for their May Eve celebration and had erected a massive maypole in the town square. Music and dancing had already begun, although the night's festivities had still not reached their apex. Arkhamites were slowly heading toward the square, many of them beneath the safety of an umbrella or protected beneath the hood of a cloak or top hat. None, though, paid the carriage any undue attention. Nor did they seem aware of the conflict occurring within.

Hawley scanned the gathering crowds and walkways for the familiar face of Louise LeMarché, but she was either not present or well-hidden among the throng. He all but stood atop the bench, the press of time's passage rattling his nerves. He could feel the weight of each individual egg in his belly, clotting his throat. Fists pounded on the wall at his back—shrill, young voices demanding to be let out.

Not knowing where else to turn, he directed the horses to return to the tavern where he and Post were boarding. She had suggested their paths would cross again, and he prayed it was soon.

Fate, it would appear, was with Salem Hawley on that fog-haunted evening, despite the lashing downpour and the sudden bucking of the carriage so ferocious, it threatened to topple the entire stagecoach, horses and all. The urchins were screaming, howling ungodly noises and swears that belied their ages but no doubt lent much credence to the harshness of their living.

"Get away from me, you motherfucking cunt!" one voice shouted.

"No!" another rang out, repeating the simple command, as if he were chiding a dog. "No! No, you stay back!" The child began to scream, then his directions cut off mid-sentence as his words were replaced with mad, soul-piercing shrieking.

Lights from the tavern and inn glowed so dully through the soupy fog that Hawley nearly overshot his mark and had to jerk on the reins to pull the horses to a halt. A painful tug within his gut bent him over double as he swung his legs over the side to step down. Post, at least, appeared to be equally ill, and Hawley realized the man was moaning, his face arched with poor humor. He hadn't noticed Post's noises over the cacophony coming from within the carriage, but the doctor was beginning to gripe more loudly of his aching belly.

"Mr. Hawley!" a familiar voice cut through the storm, followed by an earth-shaking roar of thunder and a flash of lightning. "Mr. Hawley!" she shouted again, and when Salem turned toward the female caller, he saw her dashing from the inn, careless of the foul weather and waving a hand overhead to catch his eye.

"Ms. LeMarché!" Greatly relieved, he extended a hand toward her. Before he could properly greet her, the carriage rocked on its side wheels as something within slammed into the wall. More screaming and savage utterances were carried to them on a freezing wind—then silence.

Save for the storm and the occasional complaint from Post, all was unnervingly quiet. Hawley swallowed, the back of his tongue clicking against a throat thick with contaminants.

"What has happened?" LeMarché demanded.

Hawley merely shook his head and motioned for her to step back. When he judged her to be a suitable distance away, and against the entirety of his better judgement, he stepped to the carriage door and pulled it open.

The interior of the stagecoach was akin to an abattoir. Blood was splattered across all four walls, the floor, and the ceiling; the benches were painted a blackish crimson. In the midst of it all were the children, or what little remained of them. Several of the small bodies had burst apart like rag dolls torn at the seams, and organs had spilled forth on red rivers. Those that did not appear to have exploded had been torn apart to achieve similar effect. Pulpy remains of skin and offal clung to the carriage walls, combining with the bloody remodeling to give the small traveler's space the appearance of an eccentric stucco finish.

In the center of the mess were dozens of bleating creatures feasting upon the remains, their whitish green flesh skeined in red and clumps of the innards they had birthed themselves through. As the small—and Hawley hesitated to think of them as *infants*—monstrosities swallowed, their eyes blinked. The orbs dipped into the bulging hollows of their sockets, in frog-like fashion, as if the mere act of swallowing required total use of the entire cranium.

Momentarily, Hawley was lost in the fascinating nature of their utter repulsiveness. He then came to his senses, lowering his hand to his waist for his blade, only to meet the coarse fabric of his trousers. Of course, his weapons had been seized from him.

LeMarché strode up, gaming her way between the open door and Hawley's muscled frame with a gasp. She pulled him away, one hand stealing beneath her cloak and returning with a familiar vial to splash the clear—and quite familiar smelling—liquid within the carriage. A match was produced in short order, protected beneath a cupped hand, and tossed inside. She slammed the door shut as flames engulfed the interior, feasting upon the lantern fuel and the horrors trapped within.

"We have not much time," LeMarché said. "Quickly now. You must tell me everything."

Post loosed a pained gasp, doubling over with both arms wrapped around his belly, his mouth working futilely to suck in air. His cheeks were red, and he stumbled forth on shaking knees. LeMarché went to his side, and Hawley the other.

"I fear we have even less time than you had supposed,"
he said.

LeMarché ignored Post's writhing and moaning. The man
had nearly torn himself loose from their grips halfway up the
stairs, and they'd had to carry him, wary of flailing limbs, to
get him into his room and in bed. Hawley, having gone to his
room and quickly returned, watched nervously, his fingers
tapping a staccato beat against the bone-handle hunting knife
slung through his belt loop, a flintlock gripped tightly in his
other sweaty hand.

The woman, meanwhile, busied herself at Post's dresser,
an array of brown- and green-tinted bottles set before her
atop the cabinet. She worked through a recipe she refused to
share, not even pausing to answer Hawley when he asked
what was inside the glassware. She added several drops from
each bottle into a single teacup then pulled a flask from
within her coat. From across the small room, Hawley could
smell the resultant concoction, and it burned his nose hairs.

She turned quickly, thrusting the teacup in his direction.
"Drink it."

"What is it?" he demanded.

"There's no time, Mr. Hawley. Now drink."

Frowning against the strong odor, he tossed back the
cup's contents and doubled over, gagging. Heat strong

enough to have come from the heart of Hell's own furnace burned down the length of his throat and settled deep within his belly. Sweat rose instantly across his forehead, and he immediately felt feverish, his body suddenly an oven.

Then those things within him began to pop. A churlish, acidic flavor rose into the back of his mouth. He darted to the waste pot. His knees hit the floor hard as his entire weight crashed down and his legs went out beneath him. The stench of Post's urine and feces hit him immediately, but even that was nearly pleasant in comparison to what he had only just consumed and the lingering malodorous taste it had left behind. He wretched, and a wash of thick fluid mottled with smallish gray lumps ejected from him. He vomited for what felt like an eternity, and by the time he was finished, he was entirely spent. His flesh an ashy gray, he fell to the side and lay flat on the floor.

Beside him, Post arched his back quite severely, his hips bucking off the bed so that he was supported only by his heels and shoulders. LeMarché rushed to the doctor's side and tore away the man's shirt, a grim look set upon her.

Hawley turned to see. From within Post's belly, many small webbed hands clearly pressed against the flesh. He recalled seeing a similar effect on a pregnant woman, her unborn child kicking from within the womb and pushing at the woman's stomach. Seeing such a thing occur to a man was a strange thing, and to know what was within him was all the worse.

"The drink—"

LeMarché shook her head. "He is out of time."

"What do we do?"

"End it," she said simply.

Hawley spit into the waste pot once more then cleaned his mouth with a shirtsleeve. His whole body shook, but he forced himself to his feet. When he raised his arm, miraculously, he was able to aim the flintlock steadily.

Hours ago, he had sworn to kill this man. He hadn't expect the man's murder to be a mercy upon him.

Post's eyes darted to him, the fear apparent, as was the knowledge of what was to come. Cords stood on end all along the doctor's long neck, his skull arching backward as he slammed his head into the pillow time and time again. His fingers clawed at his stomach, his nails drawing long red trenches into his skin.

Hawley stepped forward, refusing to miss even as Post writhed in bed, and pressed the barrel of the flintlock to the man's temple. He pulled the trigger, and the opposite side of Post's skull smattered against the wall.

Still, the job was not done. All along Post's torso, alien limbs pressed against the flesh, stretching the skin out, pushing it farther and farther, so that the skin tented into white peaks. They pushed and pressed until the body's elasticity finally failed and the skin snapped apart, then the creatures ripped free of his shell.

Hawley raised his blade and sent it down again and again. LeMarché was beside him, thrusting at the crater of Post's body with a long, slim silver dagger stained with brackish crimson. Small frog-like faces leered up from the pit of Post's belly, darting up beneath the man's rib cage, where LeMarché's blade followed. Eggs popped open from between the crevices of coiled intestine. The youth within broke free, already fighting for survival. The room stank of shit and copper, this on top of the perpetual and fetid mustiness of their lodgings, and Hawley tasted it all, the heat within him all-consuming. He was beyond exhausted, and yet, he matched LeMarché strike for strike.

Post's hollowed carcass was the resultant mess of unskilled and savage butcherers. His bed was soaked in waste and blood. The walls, floor, and even the ceiling were spattered in gore, as were Hawley and LeMarché. Of Dagon's children, none remained.

Hawley's knees turned to rubber, and he sank to the floor, his back to a filthy wall as he slid down. LeMarché appeared to still have some wits about her and dropped upon a nearby chair. Flecks of gray skin clung to the curls of hair on either side of her face, her porcelain skin marbled with red.

"What did you give me?" Hawley asked. Although his stomach was still unsettled, he felt better than he had in some hours. The eggs were gone from him, he could tell. His throat felt blistered, yet unplugged.

"A simple tonic meant to burn out the infestation within you."

"I do believe it worked."

"If it hadn't, you be in much similar shape as Dr. Post by now."

"This was their plan, then. To send us back here and unleash these monstrosities upon Arkham."

"Indeed. The two of you, the urchins—you were little more than bombs."

"We were meant to be sacrifices to Dagon."

"He told you that?" LeMarché said, pointing her chin toward Post's remains.

Hawley nodded. "I foolishly believed I was sent here to recover *Al Azif*, but I was blind to the real machinations. I was…" Hawley waved a hand at Post. "We both were meant to be nothing more than sacrifices."

LeMarché studied Hawley intensely for a moment before speaking again. "What else did Post say?"

"That Ellery was to use *Al Azif* to restore Dagon, and in turn herself and her own people, to their proper stations here on Earth. She seeks to resurrect her god."

"Such a thing requires more than a handful of sacrificial souls, my dear Mr. Hawley," LeMarché said, her voice grim and quiet. "You and your traveling companions were merely the beginning, I fear."

From outside, the noise of revelry, music, and merriment caught Hawley's ears, the sounds muffled by rain and occasionally lost beneath the concussion of thunder, only to be revived with a stronger fervor. The May Eve celebrations had begun in earnest.

"Their timing was quite appropriate, I see," she said, half to herself. Then she chuckled. "We must go, Mr. Hawley. It seems there is indeed no rest for the wicked."

Hawley struggled to his feet, his head spinning still from the strange elixir.

As they rushed down the staircase, heedless of their manic appearances, the celebratory excitement grew louder and louder. Then the screaming began.

Chapter 6

THEIR PALE-GREEN BODIES cut smoothly through the Miskatonic, deep beneath the storm-churned surface, until the time came to breach the river and wade ashore. Clouds covered the moonlight, and they swiftly stormed the beachhead, clinging to the shadows of the rocky outcroppings and crags of stone. Songs and revelry drew them forth, away from the river and up the bluffs overlooking the wild river. Pointed nails drove into the bluish-gray clay of the bluff face as the children of Dagon climbed hand over foot, scaling the shallow walls. Within moments, they rose atop the crest of soil and again made landfall. They came by the hundreds.

The first to notice them was Delvinia Harris, a willowy redhead in her early twenties. She was nude and on her hands and knees in the mud. The man thrusting into her from behind was not her husband, for he was beside her, with Madeline O'Mare riding atop him. Delvinia and Madeline lay close enough to kiss, and they did so, their necks and bodies straining to make contact as their swapped mates bore into them.

May Day was a time for celebration, but also an evening where mankind's most naturalistic tendencies were allowed to roam untethered in honor and celebration of Aphrodite more than the blessed Saint Walpurga. Sometimes, the old ways were better, or so it had been decided. Spring, after all, was a time of renewal, and May Day was to celebrate new growth and fertility. For this one night, married couples were allowed to remove their wedding rings, and with it their vows, and to allow their passions to grow enflamed and roam unfettered. What better way to celebrate the death of winter and the birth and renewal of life than with the spreading of seed?

In the field all around the writhing and bucking forms of the Harris and O'Mare couples, many more bodies ground together, finding pleasure among one another in the muddy, rain-soaked clearing overlooking the Miskatonic. Liquor flowed, and bottles were passed, as were, frequently, partners and mates, in a constantly shifting tableau of booze and bodies.

Delvinia watched as Harriet Duskine pleasured two men at once, wondering if perhaps Harriet would be interested in her company again. They had found themselves to be suitable partners in previous bacchanals, and the young woman was growing increasingly beautiful, as well as more skilled in lovemaking, with each passing season. Delvinia's eyes roamed the damp, moon-kissed curves of Harriet's buttocks and up the slope of her back, entranced by the puckering of her lips as her head moved back and forth over the farmer Edward Wixley's erection. She felt herself on the verge of orgasm as Mr. O'Mare drove deeper into her, and she tilted back her head in excitation, a moan boiling up inside her.

Then she saw the flash of movement, a rapid dash of quicksilver against the darkness. Her eyes sprang open as claws raked across her face. Her assailant grabbed a fistful of her hair, savagely hauling Delvinia to her feet. O'Mare stumbled away from her, and she felt suddenly empty, the shock of what was happening still barely reaching her. Her hair was tugged at again, snapping her head back to expose her neck, and then an oily mouth was upon her throat. She screamed as daggers bit into her skin, until her throat was removed and she could scream no more. Nails stabbed into her abdomen, then a hand sank agonizingly deep into her guts. She fell backward, even as her innards were pulled forward and splattered in the mud between her feet. Harriet, she saw, had a new gang of men surrounding her, much larger than the previous and far less human. She did not seem to be enjoying their ministrations half as much, and in her dying moments, Delvinia thought simply, *Tis a shame.*

Screaming erupted all across the field as lovers broke apart, darting through the grassy clearing. The children of Dagon ran them down, tackling them into the mud, claws tearing away flesh from faces, carving open backs and necks, opening up torsos, and gutting the men and women of Arkham as if they were little more than freshly caught fish.

Rain lashed down upon them all, churning the muddy, bloodstained earth. Over the clearing hung the stink of ozone, of wet earth, of copper, and of fresh offal. Husbands and wives rediscovered one another as they sought to escape, some fleeing hand in hand, their clothes and new mates all but forgotten, but it was no use. The land they had sought to fertilize with bodily pleasures had become a blood-soaked killing field, and they realized, too slowly, that there was no escape. Talons flashed, and teeth were bared as Dagon's offspring did their work, cutting through the clearing with speed and ferocity in equal measure.

Elsewhere, on the outskirts of town, Arkhamites began to take notice of the screaming reaching them from the bluffs, recognizing it now for something more primal. The tenor and pitch of the yelling was far from celebratory. It carried with it pain, horror, and fear. Too late, they realized something was terribly, terribly wrong.

Warming himself near a bonfire, Kevin Shea raised a bottle of rye to his lips as a wail of agony cut through the fog of drink. His sluggish brain responded and turned his body in time for three pointed digits to slash across his face and cleave skin and muscle from the bone of his skull. His face was cut to ribbons, one eye gone, then he fell back into the fire. His clothes, now soaked in spilled rye, caught fire immediately. He screamed as flames engulfed him. His hair burned as his body gave more fuel to the bonfire, then shock carried him into the void.

Others were less fortunate as the frog-like monstrosities took keener interests in the agony of their victims. Lydia Fryle put her back to the demons, her very first instincts propelling her into flight, but before her feet could carry her far, a hand snapped forward and grabbed her by the long, shoulder-length curls of shimmering black hair and reeled her back. Her bare feet slipped in the mud, and she fell with a startled scream. Before she even knew what was happening, she found herself pinned between two of the frogmen, their claws slicing through her garments and the flesh beneath with ease.

"No," she shouted, over and over again. "Please, no!"

Blood soaked her clothes and streamed down her figure in rivers that grew from scores of distributaries carved into her flesh. She screamed as the frogmen savaged her, hard enough that a muscle somewhere in her throat stretched and popped. Claws sank into her belly, slicing apart her innards, while teeth found her flesh. She choked on blood and bile, praying that her earthly torment was soon to be over. Eventually, Lydia's screaming halted, even as the demons continued to assail her still body.

Morgan Tanner was no less fortunate, even as he reached the edge of the clearing. He had been enjoying quality time with Tracy Sanders, the preacher's daughter. The musk of her sex was still fresh in his nostrils; his mustache and beard were wet with her excitations. The taste of her on his tongue lingered, but only her blood covered his naked body, the warmth of it dissipating in the rain. His heart was racing, driven by fear rather than the thrill of Tracy's touch. His toes sank into mud. His thin legs propelled him over the soaked earth. He could just make out the lantern lights and the shouts of revelry as pain ignited in his shoulders. Nails buried into the hollows behind each collarbone, hauling him off his feet. His back slammed into the mud. A fishlike mouth opened eagerly, revealing rows upon rows of teeth. The creature's eyes were bulbous lumps jutting from its face, without a shred of compassion or even a trace of joy. They were eyes of the dead. Morgan Tanner watched with an equal amount of dispassion as he lay there, weak and nearly drained, while the eyes blinked in time with the creature's swallowing. Those teeth ripped loose Tanner's throat, then the creature slurped down the thick chunk of meat and loose tendrils of gristle. As the darkness claimed him, his soul was weighed and measured to determine an eternity in either heaven or hell. He hoped that wherever he awoke, it would be beside Tracy and that she would smile to see him again.

Lightning flashed, slicing the sky in half for a heartbeat and turning, briefly, the creatures' black eyes an ethereal blue. The stench of loosed innards and spilled blood hung in the misty air, an odor strong enough to taste and cause even the stoutest of stomachs to turn and the hardened, leatheriest faces to blanch. A gust of wind carried the stench into the village square ahead of the children of Dagon, and it was by these smells of rot and ruin that their presence became known. By then, it was much too late, and the sounds of revelry and harmony were replaced with the screams of terror and the agonizing, pleading cries of the dying.

Chapter 7

SCREAMS TORE THROUGH THE walls and windows of the tavern as Hawley and LeMarché descended the stairs. Already those lining the bar and seated at the tables inside were taking notice of the commotion, turning their attention toward the outside.

"What's happening out there?" was the question on everyone's lips, but few had actual answers. Men began to stand and crowd around the windows, trying to spot the cause upsetting the celebratory ruckus.

"The village is under attack," LeMarché said flatly.

"All of you," Hawley said loudly, commanding the attention of each and every patron, "must take up arms immediately."

He brandished his own flintlock in one hand. In the other was a bone-handle knife, its grip warm and comfortable in his palm, like the touch of an old lover. His heart was pounding, yet he felt oddly calm. He supposed it was because he had the benefit of knowing what waited for him beyond the tavern's entrance and the grim certainty that, one way or another, this particular threat and his involvement with it would come to an end this May Eve.

Pale faces stared at him. Some rejected his words out of hand. Others seethed at the colored man's presumption to demand and bark orders at his betters, and their drunken eyes clouded over with sudden anger. They ignored LeMarché entirely, reserving a certain open aggression for Hawley.

Stay in here and die as cowards, then, he thought, but knew better than to say. His actions had already caused enough offense and broken too many closely held taboos, and the glares he received told him clearly that it would be better for his health in the near term for him to remember his place. He recalled too well similar angry eyes set in the hard faces of white soldiers who would rather die than take the advice of a black man, their stubborn pride and sense of superiority carrying them headlong into musket fire and the grave beyond. He seethed now beneath the withering stares of these white men, but he cared more for the larger, far more pressing issues of the moment.

Hawley pushed through the worrying crowd, weapons at the ready. His shoulders brusquely parted the gathering of men on either side, and he felt ungentle hands slapping at his back along the way, pushing him even as they attempted to trip him. A promise of violence hung in the air, mistakenly placed upon Hawley rather than the danger outside. If the men wanted to fight him, then so be it. *Best to do it outside, though, and quickly,* he thought. If they wanted to follow with their dander raised, then they were welcome.

LeMarché cajoled her way through the press of men as Hawley threw open the tavern doors. A blast of cold rain riding the buffeting wind smacked his face. He took a breath, comforted by LeMarché's presence at his side, then strode across the threshold and down the steps.

His booted feet sank into mud. In no time at all, his clothes became soaked through. How anybody had been able to muster a sense of festivity in such god-awful weather was beyond him, but perhaps the Arkhamites were used to it. Or maybe the villagers looked for any reason to muster some excitement and celebration, given the dreariness of daily life in Arkham, with its perpetual rain and gray skies. They had not only adapted to whatever nature threw their way, but embraced it, and on this May Eve, they had spread their arms too wide and been too inviting. Now they were being punished for it.

Moving beyond the light spilling through the tavern's windows, Hawley stepped into what he could only describe as a war zone. The street was littered with mauled and gutted bodies. Carriages had been toppled, the steaming entrails of their rent horses left to cool beneath the rain. Men and women fought and grappled with the fierce creatures, their merriment forgotten entirely as they struggled to stay alive. Those who could escaped into the houses on either side of the wide passageway, seeking safety and taking up arms. The screams that filled the night were occasionally interrupted by gunfire as the villagers grew aware of the threat and fought the monstrous plight.

Hawley raised his flintlock, taking careful aim, and put a musket ball through the soft, meaty face of a frogman loping his way. Rather than waste precious time reloading the gun, he swung his knife into the mass of creatures pressing in on him, the blade punching into one's skull. He jerked the weapon free and turned toward another one of the abominations, careful to not put his back to any of the horrors.

An awful thrill rushed through him as the blackest chamber of his soul reminded him of an awful truth, one he had thought suppressed since the war's end. Salem Hawley was a killer. He had tried to escape that fact, putting both time and distance between himself and the Revolution. Now, little more than a decade past and in the midst of a fresh battlefield, he could deny it no longer. Rather, he met it with a degree of revelry, consumed by bloodlust.

To the third creature, he swung his blade, burying it deep into the center of the thing's chest. The weapon crunched through bone and broke apart the heart hidden in the middle of it all. The shock wave riding up Hawley's arm put a tingle deep in his elbow. The blade came free on an arc of blood, and he swung again, chopping into the monster's neck and shoulder. Its puckered mouth worked frantically, uselessly, as it expired.

Shots rang past as men opened fire from within their homes and the small shops on either side of the road. Wind and rain swept away the gun smoke, but not the smell of spent cartridges and burnt powder. Most of the shooters missed their marks entirely, while a few struck the bodies of their friends and neighbors. Hawley watched helplessly as a handful of people fell to friendly fire and the marauding creatures instantly seized the opportunity to kill and feed.

His pulse quickened as he strode deeper into the mess of grappling bodies, knife swinging. During the Revolution, he had fought for his independence, and now he fought entirely for his life, with a small zeal toward revenge. He was happy to cut down the abominations, and the shrill cries of agony sent a thrill through him.

Ichor splashed his skin and stained his clothes, and he fought with the unrelenting savageness of his youth. He buried his blade into skulls and chests and slit throats wide with its sharpened edge, deep enough to decapitate. His vision was narrowed to the foe directly before him, the edges of his sight rimmed with red, and he waded through this tunnel, swinging and chopping, fighting for all his worth. Claws swiped at him, gouging his cheeks, and he swung in response, burying his knife into the center of one abomination's skull. He savagely cut downward, splitting the creature's face in half like a melon. Hawley stared into the dark cavity, seeing only a webwork of soft, hollow bones before black blood flooded the chambers of its cranium and it fell back, dead.

Musket fire erupted on either side of him, and he felt the bodies press upon him. Whatever rallying cries those men shouted, it was like hearing them from deep beneath the water. White men rushed past him, armed with rifles fastened with bayonets. Others held flaming torches, and others still had little more than kitchen knives and silver forks. He had to give the latter some credit, at least, for attempting to mount a defense, even if they were mustering themselves with such frivolous and useless arms. They could take an eye or two, he supposed. If they were to die, at least it would be a death borne of some small measure of valiancy.

The fog of war grew ever thicker, and his vision narrowed dangerously with each fresh kill. He sensed movement to his left, his reflexes responding in the nick of time to raise an arm as a tongue lashed out at him. The too-long muscle caught his jacket sleeve and wrapped around his forearm. Before Hawley could raise the knife and sever the tongue from its owner, the monstrosity leapt, his legs bowing then springing forward. Its arms came ahead, then its solid body impacted his own, sending him to the ground. They rolled together, their limbs caught up in one another, and his back hit mud, the thing atop him.

Rain splashed off the creature's whitish-green skin and stung Hawley's face. He jerked his arm, pulling the frog's tongue taut as he got a hand around it. The muscle was rough and hot in his palm and against his fingers. The thing seemed to realize Hawley's intent and bent toward him, lighting fast. Rather than chop into its tongue, his blade met the side of the frogman's face, splitting wide its cheeks and sinking into the bone beneath one eye. The creature howled fiercely, blood washing down its face. Hawley still had it by the tongue, and he yanked viciously. The frog thing fell forward, sliding off Hawley and into the mud. Salem moved fast, yanking his knife free, and mounted the creature's back. He raised the blade overhead and slammed it down into the creature's deformed skull. The way its brains poured free reminded Hawley of cutting into jelly.

Lightning flashed nearby, much too close, its brightness blinding. Reflexively, Hawley turned toward it and saw Louise LeMarché standing at the center of a crackling blue glow. Vertical strands of lightning flashed out from around her. The vines of electricity snapped away from her with a wave of her arms, whipsawing through the amphibious creatures pouncing toward her. Their wet bodies burst in a flash, feet and fingertips exploding as the current arced through them and conducted into the ground. Their skin crackled as flesh popped and the muscles beneath were cooked instantly. The stink of rotten fish clogged his nostrils. LeMarché's lips moved, but Hawley heard not a sound from her as she worked her magic.

The air filled with static, the hairs on the nape of his neck and along his hands and fingers responding to the attraction. A crisp, burnt odor hung in the air, strong even over the ruinous stink of slaughtered frogs and their jellied remains. As Hawley cut them down with his blade, LeMarché fried them in currents of lightning. Her magic, though, appeared to be weakening, and he wondered how greatly she was taxed. His mother's own magic had carried a toll, and even something as slight as a poultice took a fee from the witch's body. In order to create, one had to give.

In the bright glow of her elemental charms, the soft creases etched into LeMarché's face seemed to deepen. The gentle laugh lines around either side of her mouth were harsher, the skin on her cheeks sagging ever so slightly, and her eyes were sunken and surrounded by dark rings.

"To the harbor," she shouted.

With a ferocious crack of light, the street cleared. Smoking husks lined the avenue, and Hawley and the men courageous enough to fight in the open seized the break in action to reload their flintlocks and rifles.

"We have to get to the harbor," LeMarché said, softer this time as she leaned against Hawley for support. "That's where we will find her and that damnable book."

His weapon primed, Hawley put his arm around the witch's waist, helping her to move. Although he could not see any visible wounds, the woman carried a fresh fragility that was bone-deep. One leg was locked in place by an unbending knee so that with each step, she had to drag the limb behind her. He knew then with deadly certainty how taxing her magic had been. She had sacrificed a great deal of her own life force to ward off the demonic attackers. Looking around at the mangled, twisted remains of Arkhamites, the devastated corpses the frogmen had left in their wake, Hawley could not help but think that her efforts had been unnecessarily expensive.

"We must go." Her eyes were fixed onto a distant point far past the banks of the Miskatonic, where the river emptied into the Jersey Reef. Through the thick, curling fog and the slashing rain, the lighthouse beacon was little more than a muted period of light. It flashed, darkened, then flashed again.

Then the minor light trembled and shook as an explosion rocked the heavens, stopping Hawley in his tracks. The beacon's light fluttered and darkened as the lighthouse tower tumbled toward the earth. Great waves erupted in the distance as the stonework and masonry crashed into the water with thunderous applause.

Hawley's mind reeled. His feet were frozen despite LeMarché's insistent tugging. *What could possibly have destroyed such a grand structure?* he wondered.

A series of lightning flashes revealed the answer, and his mouth hung agape. An enormous leviathan cut through the bay, its vast serrated fin slicing neatly through the water. It reached the outcropping of land and leapt forth from the ocean, rising atop the remains of the ruined tower. With thickly muscled arms and massive clawed hands, it pulled itself out of the reef and toward the heavens. It possessed no legs. Its torso instead twisted into hundreds of impossibly long tentacles that, even as it reached the broken top of the lighthouse, never left the water. In another flash, Hawley saw its slate-colored face and the single overlarge green eye in the center of its skull. Its gigantic head swiveled slowly on a thick neck, as if the creature were surveying its kingdom. Hundreds of antennae writhed across its skull, seemingly of their own accord. The cyclopean horror roared, then the lightning wrapped the figure, exposing its nightmarish maw of teeth. Another bone-shaking bellow followed, then the creature leapt off the lighthouse, diving back into the bay with a splash so large, it sent a tidal wave breaking across the reef.

"We're too late," LeMarché said, her voice hollow. She sagged, and it was all Hawley could do to prevent her from falling into the muck.

"What is it?" he asked, although he suspected he knew all too well what the creature was.

Her words confirmed it. "Dagon. They have summoned Dagon."

Chapter 8

WAVES SLAMMED THE BANKS of the harbor like massive fists pummeling the docks. As the storm grew in intensity, so did the enormous strength of the waves. Water crashed down atop a herring fleet, several hundred ships strong, snapping masts and severing the ropes fastening the sails down, sending the great sheets of canvas airborne. A violent crest rose beneath a scallop boat, hurling it toward the shore. The boat crashed into one of the harbor's many docks, splintering into a hundred pieces, and the wind carried the shrapnel toward land. A fisherman on the dock was harpooned through the middle and sent off his feet.

Another surge of waves ripped a dogger free of its anchor and slammed it into the docks. Barnacle-encrusted pylons twisted apart beneath the wide-beamed boat. A flash of lightning offered a brief glimpse of the crew situated along the deck, their work of salting and barreling the day's catch of tuna or mackerel interrupted by the far more important task of preserving their own lives. Flipped onto its side, the dogger's fifty-foot deck struck the harbor, tearing apart docks and reducing the small ships tied off to little more than kindling. The sailors above deck were tossed into the air or smashed between the ship and whatever it came into contact with. Tons of supplies and many more tons of fish burst out of the dogger's broken belly as its spine snapped. Hawley saw no further signs of the crew, but it seemed far more likely—and far more merciful—that they were dead.

Scores of fishermen returning to shore for the night to empty their nets encountered the legions of frogmen, and the docks were awash with their heated war. Men who had made a career of gibbing herring and wrestling with catches now fought on land with fishing hooks and fillet knives. Waves smashed against the breaker walls, sending smaller, weaker waves up from the shallower waters around the docks. Great fans of sea spray washed over the sailors. A life on the water and their profession of raising creatures from the deep left them heartily inured to nature's fury. Still, the terrors they encountered here were unlike most anything they had previously seen borne from the depths of the Atlantic and the bays of Arkham. They knew enough to be scared, though, and they fought like their lives depended on it.

One fisherman took a running leap, tackling a frogman to the ground. The creature opened its mouth, and the fisherman grabbed ahold of the thing's chin with one thickly gloved hand, pushing the creature's head back to better expose its neck. His other hand was covered by a partial glove, to protect his index and middle fingers, and in this hand, he held a gibbing knife. He stabbed the blade into the monster's chin, cutting through the membrane there. Ichor ejaculated from the severed arteries, splashing against the man's chest, but he did not slow in his work. The blade arced across the membrane, and the fisherman seized ahold of this flap and wrenched it away. A gory mess of gills and entrails came loose, and he flung them to the side before resuming his cutting. Soon, the frogman stopped moving, and through the massive wound, Hawley could see the thing's spine.

Stick with what you know, his mother's voice said in his head. He nodded to himself, thinking that the fisherman had certainly done that.

"We have to find Ellery and end this madness," LeMarché said. She had to shout over the roar of the wind and waves pounding the docks. Thunder and screams polluted the air, as well, softer but no less insistent.

Whitecaps broke against the hull of the *Undaunted*. Wind punched the schooner's sails as rain lashed the decks, soaking the crew. Although the nets had been hauled in, sailors stood along the deck rails, armed with long fishing hooks and knives. The weather made pointless what few rifles they had on board, as there was no way to keep the powder charges dry during reloading. The guns would be useless after one shot, and from what they had seen of the leviathan, there was much speculation as to how effective a handful of musket balls would actually be.

The jagged crest of the massive creature's back cut through the frothing waves ahead of them. The storm violently churned the sea, but if the monster noticed it did nary much at all to slow him down. The *Undaunted* was a fast ship, its V-shaped hull and great sails cut for speed rather than safety.

Captain Bale had been a Continental Navy man in another life, having lived all his days on the sea. He'd spent many a morning in his boyhood at the Arkham wharf, watching fishing ships off the pier. After the Navy dissolved due to the Union's lack of funds, it was to those same wharves he returned as a man. He had heard grumbling about the Navy reforming in light of attacks on United States merchant ships by Barbary pirates, but unlike his schooner, Congress was a slow and lumbering machine that refused to budge even with all the world's wind at its sails. Morocco had been the first nation to recognize the United States' sovereignty, and the first to seize an American merchant ship after the nation won its independence. British treaties had kept those ships safe from the Barbary pirates, but once America was free of foreign rule, those treaties had evaporated, and their merchants were free to plunder. Bale thought it a disgrace, occasionally entertaining the idea of reenlisting should the Navy reform; other times, he thought, *The hell with it.* Life was easier on the sea during peace, even during such a hellacious day of fishing as this had brought. He'd seen war, and he'd seen peace. Only a fool actively sought war, Bale thought.

Bale knew, too, that he was a damn, bloody fool. He couldn't deny the thrill that came with chasing a quarry, and ploughing the seas before him was the largest game he had ever seen. He only wished he had a deck full of cannons around him, but hooks and blades would have to suffice.

He and his crew had watched helplessly as the gigantic beast appeared from the depths and laid waste to the lighthouse. A hostile vibe thrummed through the air itself, and a single glance in the creature's direction was enough to send pinpricks of pain behind Bale's eyes. A pulsing ache had taken root deep inside his skull, hammering at his brain with each heartbeat. Looking at his uneasy crew, he could tell these physical effects did not only affect him. Stunned, they saw it spring off the ruins, heading toward the reef. It was imperative the monster not make it to shore, and they took up chase without hesitation.

The *Undaunted* drew ever nearer, until it finally drew abreast of the black glistening fins jutting up from the water. Waves smashed against the creature's hide. Spray soaked the crew gathered along the deck, and the saltwater stung his eyes. The air felt thicker and grew damningly humid in the monster's wake, the pressure increasing tenfold to press down upon his body. Bale's headache grew all the stronger, and he winced against the steady throbbing. He pushed his way through the men and gripped the deck railing to study the beast. It was large, far larger than he had realized, although he knew it must have been massive judging from the ease with which it had destroyed the lighthouse. Even still, his mind struggled to cope with the sheer enormity of such a find.

"Now!" he screamed into the bleeding ear of the closest sailor. His command was carried over the torrent and down the line on either side of him. Thoughtlessly, he brushed at his own ear and caught sight of a streak of red on the back of his hand before it was washed away by seawater.

The men went to work, thrusting their long spears over the side of the boat and stabbing at the gargantuan squid-like creature beneath them. The spear tips scratched uselessly at the flesh of the hump, but the sailors continued to stab, over and over.

A wave rose ahead of them, breaking over the bow to briefly flood the deck. Cold water snatched at Bale's ankles, filling his boots and freezing his feet. His hand darted out reflexively to help a nearby fisherman keep his feet, grabbing the back of his coat before the man could be tossed overboard. Water lurched beneath the hull, tossing the *Undaunted* into the air. As the boat crashed through the tidal fist and punched back down onto the reef, more water splashed across the deck.

"Keep fighting," Bale shouted. He stabbed his own spear down at the beast, but the blade glanced harmlessly across the surface of the armor-like skin. *God, what I wouldn't give for a cannon*, he thought ruefully.

Metal nipped at alien hide, but took no chunks from the creature. Bale half-suspected the thing was not even aware of their presence, but before the thought could fully form, he saw a massive green orb turn toward them from beneath the dark currents. Even through the heavy chop and watery distortion, he couldn't help but think the behemoth was looking right at him. Then a wave raised the *Undaunted*, breaking their eye contact.

Bale gripped the railing, his knuckles white, as the ship continued to rise. Salt water peeled off the deck, and a moment later, the schooner crashed back down. Water rained upon them, and it took a moment for his brain to assemble the sights laid out before him into a comprehensible image. Somehow, he'd found himself standing in the center of a waterfall as the water pounded against him in a thick, heavy sheet, facing a slick, moss-covered rock wall. Then the wall shifted, the skin rippling. He realized the creature was standing before him, the Atlantic Ocean sliding off its body to rain down upon the deck of the *Undaunted*.

One of the men screamed, and Bale turned in time to see the sailor torn off his feet, a thick appendage wrapped tightly around him, leaving only his head and one foot exposed. The tentacle tightened, twisting around the body, which then popped loudly. A shower of blood sheeted over Bale, and one of the sailor's boots fell to the deck. A moment later, a pulped mash slammed down. The man's shattered head hung wilting on a broken frame.

More tentacles rose, grabbing the *Undaunted* and hauling it out of the water. Men were tossed off their feet. A sailor flew through the air and hit the hull of the dory lashed upside down to the deck, his spine snapping.

Staring up at the enormous thing, Bale felt something pop in his eyes, and his vision turned red. His sanity was slipping, as if he stood on a precipice between reality and insanity. Screams erupted beside him. He turned to see the closest fisherman clawing at his eyes, digging bloody trenches down his face, his nails stripping away the flesh of his cheeks and along his jaws. Openmouthed, Bale watched, horrified, as the man then drove his fingers into his eyes, pushing two digits into each jellied orb, popping them.

The creature reached a massive hand toward another crewman and gripped his head between two fingers. With a slight twist of its wrist, the leviathan tore loose the crewman's skull, and blood geysered out from the stump of his neck. Rain and thunder pounded the air all around them. The noise of wood creaking was barely audible beneath the violent storm and the cacophony of so many men slipping into insanity.

Screaming, thick currents of blood pouring from his nose and ears, Bale drove his spear toward one of the tentacles gripping his ship, intent on at least scratching this damnable abomination. A splintering crack sounded loudly. The beast was tightening its grip, breaking the ship apart in its constricting muscular tentacles.

Bale stabbed again, standing at an awkward angle on the slanted, ever-shifting deck, and watched helplessly as his men were torn apart. The creature opened its mouth and screamed. Bale's eardrums exploded, and he fell back, dizzy. His whole head felt as though it were cracking apart. Blood welled up in the back of his throat.

"I can't do this," a crewman said, crying blood as he positioned his spear before him. With the point situated beneath his chin, pressed against his throat, he let his knees go weak and impaled himself. The spear tip shot out the back of his neck on a jet of blood.

The *Undaunted* lurched again, and Bale fell on his back. The tentacle shifted once more. He could no longer hear the catastrophic noise of his vessel being ripped in half, but through the deck he lay on, he could feel the thrum of his ship exploding apart. Then he was falling, falling… falling.

He struck the waves feet first, his legs snapping. Saltwater flooded his mouth as he made to scream, swallowing it down in his panic. The *Undaunted* had been reduced to massive splinters, and giant shards of jagged wood hit the Atlantic all around him. He was too disoriented to swim, but the swath of ruin pouring down from the sky would have been inescapable even for a strong man with two good legs.

Above, the creature unfurled its long limb, sprinkling the messy remains of the ship and his crew into the sea. Bale looked up in time to see the creature's fingers gripping one of his sailors around the man's head and feet. The sailor was plucked apart, his entrails slipping loose of his body and free-falling through the air to splash down in the ocean. Bale felt his brain melt, turning into sludge as the throbbing pain continued to grow, and a fractured laugh erupted from him. He couldn't help but laugh.

The *Undaunted*'s bowsprit cut through the sky, its shredded sails loose and flapping uselessly in the air. The point of it impaled Bale through the chest, and his body was dragged beneath the ocean. The taste of salt and copper flooded into his mouth, and his eyes burned against the sting of the ocean. Captain Bale had always suspected he would die at sea. He was right.

The militia rallied at the wharf's edge, armed with rifles affixed with bayonets. Behind them, the pack mules drafted into service to transport artillery were whipped for their protestations. The mules were whinnying and rearing up on hind legs, kicking their forelimbs. White froth wicked away from their foaming jaws with each shake of their howling heads.

"Cut them loose and haul those cannons into place by hand then, goddamnit," one of the men shouted. His rank was impossible to determine as none of the men had bothered to dress in their uniforms. Each had been mustered and pressed into service in whatever they were wearing. For some, that meant hardly anything at all, having been enjoying their freedom from their marriage vows during the May Day celebration. Others wore garments that were virtually pasted to their bodies, so sodden were they by the storm and drink.

The mules were freed of their harnesses, and they bolted into the woods, on a trajectory that would take them away from both the bloodied shore and away from Arkham. Four-man gun crews moved the eighteen- and twenty-four-pound siege cannons into place along the bluffs, took their best aim, and set to priming. The downpour provided plenty of water to wet the spongeman's sponge, and he set about cleaning the bore. The loader pushed in a bag of powder and a metal ball, which the spongeman rammed down into the bore. The ventsman cut the bag of powder through the vent hole, and then the gun commander gave the order.

"Fire!"

Cannonballs cut across the bay, many of them striking their massive target, while others smashed harmlessly into the bay. Finding a target with such artillery was never a given, but the sheer enormity of the leviathan helped simplify matters even for an inexperienced gun crew. The great beast's skin rippled with each impact, but it continued striding through the bay unaffected, as if the cannons had done little more than merely poke at its flesh. Gun crews scrambled to reload their artillery. Their work was sloppy as panic overtook them. Riflemen squared the butts of their stock to their shoulders and took aim at the approaching waves of frogmen crossing the fields.

Pandemonium took hold, running through the ranks of fighters as they engaged their inhuman adversaries. Quickly, the battlefield was filled with gun smoke, blood, and screams cut short. A young gunner found himself impaled on the claws of a frogman, while another had his face sliced apart in one swift attack.

A rifleman stabbed at one of the abominations with his bayonet, spearing the creature through the middle, but failed to keep himself out of arm's reach. The wounded animal seized the rifleman's head in both hands and squeezed. His skull cracked apart along the lines of sutures fusing the plates of bone together. As the man's head came apart, the creature's claws dug into the man's brains, squeezing gray matter loose in thick clumps between its fingers.

The men's senses were shattered by the bellowing of the leviathan swiftly cutting through the reef toward shore. Massive tentacles whipped out of the bay, carrying with them a spray of salt water as they leeched onto the bluffs. Cannon fire met the beast but did little more than anger it. Tentacles swept across the clearing, shattering the wooden mounts and unmooring the cannons. Metal tubes were flung through the air, end over end, pulverizing any militiamen and frogmen unfortunate enough to be standing in its path.

Tentacles seized a cluster of men in their grips and squeezed them into pulp, while others lashed out and cut through one company, tearing some of the men in half or plucking loose limbs from others. A giant sucker on the underside of a tentacle swallowed a man's head whole and ripped the cranium free, the spine and jagged shards of rib bone still attached, as the limb swung violently away. The leviathan rose, and devastation followed on a tide of turmoil and agony.

"They have been seeding this land with rain," LeMarché said, "preparing the world for Dagon's arrival."

Her voice was a husky whisper, as if the very act of speaking were a fresh hell upon a tormented throat. Pressed against Hawley for support, she did not look well at all, and he could feel the change in her weight as she grew lighter.

Brilliant arcs of electricity flashed in the air, frying a handful of frogmen darting toward them from across the wharf. Their pale-green skin rippled and popped as the sudden heat of electricity flash-fried them. Half-melted, they fell to the docks. Steam rose from their baked bodies, which sizzled briefly beneath the cold rain. The creatures were everywhere, hundreds of them. More climbed out of the bay or slammed wet hands down onto the end of the boat docks to haul themselves up and out of the drink.

Smoke roiled out of one of the canneries as something within caught fire. A low rumbling shook the earth from somewhere farther down the wharf. Hawley imagined vats of fish oil catching fire and exploding, then he shook the thought loose. Enough savagery plagued Arkham without him having to invent further chaos.

Whether distracted or simply exhausted, LeMarché allowed enough of an opening for one of the creatures to leap upon them. Hawley stepped back, away from the slashing claws, and LeMarché stumbled, losing her grip on his shoulders, and struck the deck hard. Hawley swung his knife and opened the frogman's belly. Hot intestines splattered the ground beneath its feet. Another swing took off the creature's head.

He held out a hand, helping LeMarché to her feet. Her blouse was torn in three places, scarlet lines vividly etched in her flesh between the gaps of scored fabric. Blood welled in her wounds but was almost instantly washed away by the stinging rain.

"Are you able to continue?"

She nodded, her soaked hair hanging in thick, matted clumps around her wet face. "I shall have to."

Magic may have taken its toll on her physical appearance, and although she looked fragile and aged, clearly an ember of strength still burned deep within her. Hawley squeezed her closer to his body, an arm around her hip, and bore her weight. They would see this through together, and she could draw from him whatever strength she needed.

"Don't look at the beast," she warned him.

He nodded his understanding. Already, he could feel his sanity fraying. A thick gray caul of madness blanketed his mind, panic rising at its edges. Screams of agony rang out all along the wharf, but so did the cackles of insanity, the noises of men's minds snapping and breaking entirely. Nearby, a fisherman dispatched his mutant opponent then turned toward the bluffs overlooking the bay to survey the enormity of Dagon. His mouth fell open moments later as he sank to his knees. Then he turned his fillet knife toward his face and stabbed at his eyes. Merely blinding himself was not enough. As sheets of blood poured down his cheeks, he continued to stab at his face. The tip of the blade crunched through bone, over and over. He carved out a dozen new hollows in his skull before slashing his throat from ear to ear, laughing madly until, finally, a gurgle of blood drowned out the laughter.

The fisherman was not alone in his madness. All along the docks, men became either complicit in their own murders at the talons of the frog creatures or succumbed to suicide. Others turned on one another, burying their knives in each other's bodies or grappling by hand and biting one another.

"Don't look," LeMarché said again.

He kept his head down, icy rain sheeting down upon him.

LeMarché spoke her cryptic words in a hushed whisper barely audible over the storm, and streaks of lightning flashed through the air. Her attack focused its fury upon Dagon's children and crazed men alike. There was no saving the men with minds so fractured that to allow them to live a moment longer was to allow them undue torment. Burnt husks fell to the soaked planks all around them. Before long, they were striding through a battlefield littered with the dead.

Hawley recalled a similar scene as Loyalist insurgents had attacked the Rhode Island Regiment, of which Hawley had been a part, along the Croton River. Most of the regiment had been murdered, while others were captured. Some, like Hawley, had been lucky enough to avoid such a fate. Hawley had escaped into the woods, fleeing from the field littered with dead black soldiers.

Now, rather than flee for his life, Hawley strode ever deeper through the battlefield. He stepped over and around the steaming, blackened husks of the dead and made his way to the end of the wharf.

"There." LeMarché pointed a bony, curled finger toward the hooded figure standing atop a tall stone at the end of a long, rocky outcropping.

Waves crested the rocks, whitecaps rising to break against the stones and pummeling Ellery. Somehow, she stood unfazed. Half a dozen frog creatures encircled her, their movements jittery with excitation. The wind grew stronger as the storm's severity increased. Lightning cut through the sky, revealing more such creatures kneeling in supplication in the shallow waters off the shore, their faces pointed toward Dagon.

Hawley held LeMarché close as they reached the end of the wharf and climbed down off the pier, their feet sinking into tide that had risen over the beach.

LeMarché barked a surprised laugh, her fingers tightening around Hawley's forearm as the shock stole her breath. "Oh, that's cold."

Her noises interrupted the frog creature's rapture. They turned toward her and Hawley, teeth bared, and walked through the surf. Moonlight glowed against their black deadly eyes and flashed across their wickedly sharp talons. LeMarché turned her head up to find Hawley's eyes, and he saw fear—honest, pure fear—for the first time that night.

"I can't." LeMarché had no need to explain. Her weakness was readily apparent, her body having already paid a severe cost to bring them this far. She slipped free of Hawley, standing unsteadily, but miraculously, upright.

He gripped his bone-handle knife and stepped forward, moving headlong into the impending fray. Gunfire exploded in the air around him. His mouth dropped open as a trio of the frog monsters fell. Others rushed forward, and he swung his knife while freeing a second blade from his coat. Steel met the scaly, pale hides, and the screams of the unearthly creatures met his ears.

From behind, a small band of militiamen were attempting to rush, quite ungainly, through the high tide. They carried rifles affixed with bayonets, and they found bodies warm enough to bury swords in. Other men strode to just within arm's length and fired their pistols into the skulls of the enemy, then either used the small flintlocks to bash at the creatures or lashed out with knives.

"Kill all of them," the militia commander shouted. Thunder followed his words, as if he wielded the fury of nature itself. "Don't stop until every one of them is dead!"

He raised his rifle in an effort to rally the men, fresh words of encouragement on his lips. Rather than words, blood spilled over his lips. The stern look upon his face contorted into pain. Claws slashed through his belly then his throat, unzipping his neck.

Hawley was quick to avenge the fallen commander, turning on a heel to bury the blade into the distorted, fish-like face of the monstrosity. Its head split in half as if it were made of eggshell, then it slumped in a heap atop the dead militiaman.

Already, the other soldiers were rushing past, a handful of them armed with knives and hatchets for close-in work, having already spent their rifle and pistol loads. Stopping to reload would have meant certain death. Despite the commander's demise, his orders had stuck, and the soldiers trudged through the muck and the high tide toward the rocky outcropping. Frogmen swam to meet them.

"Let's get moving." Hawley put an arm around LeMarché.

Her face was pale, but her cheeks were red. She licked her lips and gave an uncertain nod. Together, they pushed their way forward.

Muddy sand sucked at Hawley's boots, threatening to bare his feet to the slick rocks beneath his soles. Somewhere along the way, LeMarché had already lost her shoes. The ground was uneven and scored with stones, but she voiced no complaints. Discomfort was etched into her face, however.

"We're almost there," he assured her.

The darkness grew deeper as Dagon shifted along the bluffs, his bulk blotting out the moon. While the majority of him was hidden by the pitch waters of the bay, his massive hands held him skyward, pressing down against the grassy clearing above the cliff. Tentacles swept across the land, picking up and throwing cannons as if they were little more than children's playthings or grabbing ahold of men and plucking them into pieces. The earth shook as Dagon climbed upon the bluffs, then the ground beneath his fingers caved in. Soaked by the constant rains, the bluffs had been greatly weakened. Rivers of mud began sheeting down the side of the cliff face, loosening the massive stones embedded in the earth, then the crest of land sledged away entirely, slipping into the bay. Men were carried down the current of mud, disappearing into the flow as they were swept away. Dagon reared back, and the ground rumbled again as it let loose a throaty bellow. Then it flung itself away from the land and back into the water, sending an enormous wave across the shore. Ships were dragged in across the reef and broken against the ground. Many more men and women of Arkham drowned.

Water flooded over Hawley and LeMarché, taking them off their feet and burying them in the deep. Hawley opened his eyes to the stinging salt, but found only darkness. He pushed aside the panic and kicked his legs, unsure which way was up or down. The air had been punched from his lungs, and they burned as he twisted beneath the water, searching for LeMarché. He nearly took in a mouthful of salt water when fingers grabbed his shoulder and pulled him around. Her hand took his, and together, they rose. Hawley sucked in air then worked to reorient himself. They had been hauled out into the bay, a good twenty yards away from shore.

He saw no sign of the militia or the frog monsters. He found the outcropping of giant rocks easily enough. The wave had dragged them closer to Ellery. Hawley was stunned to see her still standing, the tome in hand and opened as she read. But she was alone. However she had survived the massive fist of saltwater, her mutant companions had not been so lucky.

Past Ellery, a thick scaled hide rose out of the water. Tentacles on either side of it reached into the air, drifting lazily. Where water struck Dagon's back, small puffs of steam rose upon contact.

"We need that book," LeMarché said. The exhaustion in her voice was impossible to miss.

Hawley was quite sympathetic. His entire body felt like a bruised, beaten lead weight, his limbs nearly ten tons each. Despite the bone-deep tiredness and soul-breaking pain, he swam, and LeMarché swam alongside him.

Climbing the rocks covered in water and a slimy layer of moss was slow, dangerous, and exhausting. Finding a grip on this finger of land was difficult. Their soaking clothes only added to the wearying struggle, and Hawley's garments seemed intent on dragging him back down into a watery grave.

When they finally got their feet beneath them, Ellery had her back to them still. Rain fell all around her, but touched neither her nor the grimoire she read from. Her lips moved, but the words were lost beneath the storm and the crashing sounds of waves. Her wide-open eyes were oval flints staring off at a distant point rather than at the book in her hands.

Following the direction of her eyes, Hawley felt a piece of his soul break apart and sledge loose through his guts so much like the mudslide only moments ago. The night itself had been torn. The tapestry of stars on either side of the wide gash was lost in the wrinkled heavens. From somewhere deep inside this hole, he caught flashes of movement. The sky shimmered, and Hawley realized it was not the heavens above but ocean—an emerald, violent ocean filled with arcane horrors held suspended in the sky. Tentacles pressed against the caul separating their world from his own, and the caul shifted, pregnant with the movements of terrors unlike anything the Earth had known.

Without thinking, he acted, swiftly and decisively. Before Ellery could speak one more line, he swung the knife and buried the blade into the crook of her neck. Instantly, the rain found her and *Al Azif*. She turned toward him, legs already buckling as the book fell from her open palms. LeMarché reached toward *Al Azif* unsteadily, and the book fell between her hands, slamming shut upon the rocks.

Ellery looked up at Hawley with surprised eyes. Clearly, she'd had no idea he was behind her. She raised one long-fingered hand to her neck and gingerly dabbed at her wound. Her eyes widened at, but did not seem to recognize the importance of, her blood so vibrant against her green-hued flesh. She attempted to stand, but the driving rain and crashing waves pummeled her to her knees.

Hawley could stomach the sight of her no longer. Ellery raised a warding hand between them, but he shoved her arm away and lifted the knife again. He brought it down quickly. Bone split loudly beneath the blade, and a warm, sticky spray splashed across Hawley's face. He blinked the blood out of his eyes. His vision cleared in time to see Ellery collapse into a rising wave and slide off the rocks to the water below.

When he turned his attention to LeMarché, she was frantically flipping through the pages of the thick grimoire. On the verge of panic, she stopped, went back a few pages, and studied the lines there, written in a tongue Hawley did not recognize. He stood over her, hoping to shield her and the book from the rain with his body, but succeeded only in dripping upon both. Her fingers swept more pages aside as she dug deeper.

Moments later, she shouted, "Yes!" then began to read.

The words were hard and guttural. Listening to them made Hawley feel oddly violated. A sense of shame rose through him as he listened to the foreign and ancient words, although he could not explain the feeling, nor the sudden twisting of guilt upsetting his stomach, save only that he knew instinctively this language was not meant for his ears.

Lightning scored the sky, flashing across the tear above. Dagon lurked somewhere out in the sea, deep beneath the turbulent currents. There was no sign of the mammoth thing, but Hawley knew it was out there. He could still feel the strumming vibratro the creature exuded and the gray haze of insanity that foretold of Dagon itself. Hawley had to remain on guard, lest he slip into the welcoming embrace of madness. To find peace, all he would have to do was draw his knife across the backs of his forearms, from wrist to elbow, or across his neck, ear to ear, and it would all be over. His body would fall, likely into the dark recesses of the reef, and he would feel no coldness, only warmth, as if he were stepping into a lover's arms. The water would surround him as the blood welled up and out of his body and—

"No! Stop it!" he shouted at himself, railing against the cold, dark thoughts lurking within his own mind and the fantasies of his self-inflicted death.

A thousand crisscrossing arcs of lightning snapped in and out of existence across the sky, growing stronger. Then the light struck the bay, sending brilliant orbs of lightning across the water's surface. Tendrils of light reached deep into the water, a shimmering current of electricity blasting atop the waves.

Dagon rose, bands of crackling light flashing across the surface of its gigantic form, binding its arms and tentacles to either side. More lightning sizzled against its enormous body, stabbing into it like so many hooks and hauling it out of the water as if it had been caught on a fishing line.

The tear in the sky wrenched open wider as Dagon rose. The caul separating the realms bubbled as the creatures behind him caught sight of the massive beast rising toward them, and soon, the sky was still. Whatever had been behind that caul had stopped moving, had perhaps even left, fleeing from the presence of Dagon.

The leviathan screamed as more bands of electricity snapped around him, and the ocean shivered. Whitecaps crashed against the rocks before Hawley, and he raised an arm to his face, blocking the sight of Dagon and the sting of salt spray.

LeMarcé knelt on the rocks, her eyes focused on the text beneath her. Its pages had turned brown from the soaking rains, and the book was waterlogged.

Another roar shook the heavens. Hawley's hands reflexively clapped over his ears, trying to block out the sound. He fell to his knees, unable to hear his own screaming. Waves slammed against him, threatening to take him down into the drink. He slid to the side on a buffet of wind. The rocks tore open the knees of his trousers, ripping his shirt as he scrambled for purchase.

He thought about simply letting go, of letting the water have him, once and for all. And then the air stilled. The rain stopped. The water beneath him calmed itself, and the lightning storm all but vanished.

LeMarché's fingers were around his wrists, helping him to stand. The woman looked ancient, far, far older than her years. Electricity had coursed through her body, using her up, taking all it needed. Dagon was gone. The dark skies were clear and perfectly whole, unblemished and unmarked.

It's finished, he thought. *Finished at last.* He settled against the rocks, and LeMarché knelt beside him. He closed his eyes and breathed deeply of the burnt air and wet earth, of its saltiness and of the stink of rotting fish. It was a pure smell. An awful smell, but a pure one.

It's over, he thought again. For a moment, he enjoyed the lie.

Chapter 9

FOR THREE DAYS, SALEM Hawley slept. He woke only to use the waste pot, because a charley horse seized his leg, or when a particularly savage dream woke him with a startled scream. Such moments came upon him only briefly, and within minutes, his weariness and bone-deep aches hauled him back beneath the welcoming dark tides of sleep and the brief escape it afforded.

On the third day, his eyes struggled to open, but the strength of the sun was too overwhelming to ignore, even with the thick drapes drawn tightly shut. He blinked loose the gumminess binding his eyelashes together and knuckled away the rocky formations of crust that had settled into the corners of both eyelids. For a time, he merely lay there. Even in his stillness, the pain was complete, and when he dared to finally move, his muscles angrily sounded their excruciating fury. With nowhere else to be, he took his time rising, slowly folding his legs over the side of the mattress, wincing as his feet took the full weight of his damaged body. His tired legs carried him, limping with each step, to the dresser and the clothes that had been folded away inside. He paused for a moment in the glow of a sunbeam and enjoyed the heat across his bare skin, like a cat uncoiling across the floorboards to warm itself.

The pieces of his mind struggled to catch up, and some of those pieces would forever carry a jagged edge, refusing to slot in peaceably with the adjoining parts. Things were broken, shattered by the sights no human mind could reasonably tolerate or observe without fracturing. Meeting his reflection, he noticed the gray streaking his hair and speckling the dark shadows of growth along his jawline and chin.

Once dressed and warmed by a cup of black tea, he drew on his coat… and remembered. The flyer he had taken from Miskatonic was still folded inside the inner pocket where he had hurriedly shoved it, and it had been protected well from the elements.

LeMarché, he discovered in the adjoining room. Both she and Hawley had been brought to the militia's fort with the wounded soldiers and as many of the injured townsfolk as the meager medical facility could handle. The nurses and doctors were quickly overwhelmed, but they at least had a greater number of staff than the much smaller clinic in Arkham, or so Hawley recalled hearing during a brief moment of cognizance.

The French woman looked much as Hawley felt. He hardly recognized her at first. Her eyes gave it away, though, when they fell upon him and her lips curved upward. She was buried beneath a pair of blankets, the drapery drawn open wide to permit the sun to lay upon her. Even swathed in the golden rays, her skin carried a deathly pallor.

Hawley drew a chair to her side, and their hands coupled. He gave her fingers a gentle squeeze.

"You're finally awake," she said.

"I don't know how you are."

She laughed and shrugged, wincing. Briefly, she tried to shift into a more comfortable position and eventually gave up. Comfort would be an impossible discovery.

"I fear I do not have much time left," she said. When he attempted to speak, perhaps to deny her claim, she squeezed his fingers tightly to silence him. "You have been dreaming, I know. You have seen things, of both the past and of the things to come, and you have much to learn, Mr. Hawley."

He wondered how much she knew. Did his screaming wake her in strange hours of the night?

"It feels like a lifetime ago." He freed his hands to reach into his coat. "But when I was at the university, I found this."

He unfolded the paper gently, afraid that tremors seizing his hands would prompt him to tear apart the flyer in a fit of madness. He smoothed out the folds upon her lap. "In my sleep, I see an empty field of white, of ice and snow. I'm lost and wandering, and I know I am freezing to death. The wind howls across me. *Through* me. And then I see it—a black pyramid. It's off in the distance, somehow untouched by the elements, and so, so perfect."

He licked his lips, suddenly uncomfortable by the admission. "In New York, before I came here, I saw something similar. One of the men who opened this…" He had to stop and consider his words, wondering at how outlandish it all sounded. Of course, if anyone were to understand, it would be LeMarché, who herself had opened a portal and expelled an unholy creature through it.

Regardless, the words felt ill-formed upon the tip of his tongue, lumpy and nauseating. To speak of it was madness, and another edge of memory splintered, fractured, and stabbed at his mind. He rubbed at his face, slicking back his sweaty hair.

"This portal," he said finally. "They opened this portal, tore open the sky, and one of the men was pulled through. I saw snow, felt the cold and the wind. And I've been seeing it ever since, in every dream. Every night I sleep, I see it all."

She picked up the flier and read it, nodding with understanding.

"And then I saw this," he said, tilting his head toward the paper. "A call for crewmen aboard the *Calypso*."

LeMarché read the brief missive, absorbing the words Hawley had already memorized.

Men wanted: For hazardous journey. Small wages, bitter cold, long months of complete darkness, constant danger, safe return doubtful. Honour and recognition in case of success.

She smiled, but it lacked warmth and failed to shine in her eyes. "An expedition to the Arctic."

"I will be on that ship," he said with finality.

"Four months," LeMarché said, noting the date of debarkation. "A short amount of time to teach that which you will need to know." Her eyes closed as her head sank back into the pillow.

"I'm a fast learner."

A small smile curled her lips. "You'll have to be."

Her hand fell away from the paper, but the advertisement stayed flat atop the blanket. Moments later, she was asleep and snoring.

Hawley sat beside her for a long while, drawing comfort from her presence and the heat of the sun. Eventually, he took back the paper. He refolded it, hiding the artistic rendering of the *Calypso* sailing through freezing waters as men made landfall and pointed to an object far off in the distance—a black pyramid barely visible in a storm of sleet and ice.

Salem Hawley will return in

THE BLACK ROCK

Coming soon…

A note to Readers

Thank you for choosing to read this book – it is greatly appreciated, and I hope you enjoyed the journey!

If would be willing to spare a minute or two, please leave a brief review of this work and let other readers know what you thought. Reviews are incredibly helpful, particularly for an independent author and publisher such as myself, and can help determine the success of a novel. Reviews do not need to be long — twenty words or so should suffice — but their impact can be enormous.

I look forward to your thoughts, and thank you, once again, for taking the time to read this story.

If you would like to know about upcoming releases, I encourage you to subscribe to my newsletter at http://www.michaelpatrickhicks.com.

Acknowledgements

Writing a series of historical horror novellas presented a fair degree of challenges, many of which were overcome with diligent research. Despite these stories being obviously fictional, maintaining a veneer of realism was important. The saying "God is in the details" led me to search out a fair amount of small, yet highly important, details. A lie is, after all, easier to sell when surrounded by truths.

Borne of the Deep required me to dig into some details that might even strike readers as trivial. Given that so much of this novella's first act occurred during an eighteenth-century road trip, stagecoach travel was one topic of research. The Pilgrim Hall Museum's Getting There from Here exhibit and the online publication, "Journey by Land" (accessible at http://www.pilgrimhall.org/pdf/Journey_by_Land.pdf.) proved to be valuable and informative resources.

Because this book took a far deeper dive into Lovecraftian lore than the preceding volume, *The Resurrectionists*, I had to brush up on my knowledge of Dagon and the Deep Ones. I certainly took my own fair share of liberties along the way, but the Lovecraft wiki http://lovecraft.wikia.com was quite a valuable resource along the way.

Walpurgis Night is more commonly celebrated in Europe, but there's enough evidence out there that May Eve and May Day celebrations were held by European settlers who arrived on the American continent. As far as I know, Maypoles are not erected with any great frequency these days, but I suspect back in 1788, when this story is set, people were looking for any reason they could find to celebrate. They most certainly were aware of Walpurgis Night in the fictional Arkham, Massachusetts, where this is set, as May Eve is referenced in Lovecraft's *The Dreams in the Witch House*. I knew very little of Walpurgis Night going into this story, but The Dabbler brought me up to speed with their article, "May Day, Beltane, and the Menace of May Eve" (http://thedabbler.co.uk/2015/04/may-day-beltane-and-the-menace-of-may-eve/).

Researching this book was fun, and at times, I was forced to bend the truth a bit in order to serve the fiction. But for all those details I didn't get exactly right, the blame falls squarely with me. Hopefully, I did well enough that no (or at least, not too many) glaring errors were dragged kicking and screaming out of this book's dark pages.

For all the things I didn't get right in the construction of prose and wordsmithing, I can only blame myself. Thankfully, I had a small team at Red Adept Editing to help me look good and fix all the very many things I had broken. I would like to thank my editor, Stefanie Spangler Buswell, and my proofreader, Kristina B., for helping me corral this manuscript into its final, publishable form.

I can never thank Kealan Patrick Burke enough for his impeccable artworks. In addition to being an excellent cover designer, he's a damn fine writer, as well—you should be reading his books if you're not already.

Speaking of reading and writing, I want to give a shout out to the authors who have aided and/or inspired me along the way, directly or otherwise, and maybe even inadvertently on their end… I am indebted to John Hornor Jacobs, Chris Soresen, Glen Krisch, Jeremy Hepler, Tim Meyer, Hunter Shea, Chuck Buda, Todd Keisling, Somer Canon, Jonathan Janz, Brian Keene, Gabino Iglesias, V. Castro, Edward Lorn, Cullen Bunn, Kevin Watkins, Steve Stred, and Daron Kappauff for their support, retweets, Facebook shares, blurbs, comments, advice, laughs, drinks (too few and with too few of you, but we'll unfuck that eventually, I hope), podcasts, and stories along the way. Even if you don't think you helped, you did. And speaking of podcasts, thanks also to Scott Kemper and Matt Brandenburg, who allow me to co-host *Staring Into The Abyss* and talk all things horrific on a weekly basis. They have introduced me to some mighty fine works of dark speculative fiction that have slipped past my radar.

Thanks, also, to those wonderful bookstagrammers, bloggers, and reviewers who have helped promote my work to new readers, particularly Sadie Hartmann and the Night Worms crew, Jamie, Tony, Toni (both of you!), Mindi, Laurie, Emily, Tracy, Alex, the Davids, Lilyn, Shane, Jim, Char, and all the rest. You all rock, and don't think I haven't noticed.

Finally, thank *you*, dear reader, for giving this work a shot. I hope you enjoyed this story. Your support is very much appreciated, and it helps keep me going.

See you all at the Black Rock.

ABOUT THE AUTHOR

Michael Patrick Hicks is the author of several horror books, including *The Resurrectionists, Broken Shells: A Subterranean Horror Novella,* and *Mass Hysteria.* He co-hosts Staring Into The Abyss, a podcast focused on all things horror. His debut novel, *Convergence,* was an Amazon Breakthrough Novel Award Finalist in science fiction. He is a member of the Horror Writers Association.

In addition to his own works of original fiction, he has written for the online publications Audiobook Reviewer and Graphic Novel Reporter, and has previously worked as a freelance journalist and news photographer in Metro Detroit.

Michael lives in Michigan with his wife and two children. In between compulsively buying books and adding titles that he does not have time for to his Netflix queue, he is hard at work on his next story.

For more books and updates on Michael's work, visit his website and subscribe to his newsletter at http://michaelpatrickhicks.com

CHECK OUT THESE
OTHER TITLES FROM

HIGH FEVER
BOOKS

MICHAEL PATRICK HICKS

BROKEN SHELLS

BROKEN SHELLS

Antoine DeWitt is a man down on his luck. Broke and recently fired, he knows the winning Money Carlo ticket that has landed in his mailbox from a car dealership is nothing more than a scam. The promise of five thousand dollars, though, is too tantalizing to ignore.

Jon Dangle is a keeper of secrets, many of which are buried deep beneath his dealership. He works hard to keep them hidden, but occasionally sacrifices are required, sacrifices who are penniless, desperate, and who will not be missed. Sacrifices exactly like DeWitt.

When Antoine steps foot on Dangle's car lot, it is with the hope of easy money. Instead, he finds himself trapped in a deep, dark hole, buried alive. If he is going to survive the nightmare ahead of him, if he has any chance of seeing his wife and child again, Antoine will have to do more than merely hope. He will have to fight his way back to the surface, and pray that Jon Dangle's secrets do not kill him first.

"A fun and nasty little novella...If you're a big creature-feature fan (digging on works like Adam Cesare's *Video Night* or Hunter Shea's *They Rise*) you're going to love this book."
- **Glenn Rolfe, author of *Becoming* and *Blood and Rain***

"Lightning fast...high octane fun."
- **Unnerving Magazine**

"An adrenaline-fueled, no punches pulled, onslaught of gruesome action! Highly recommended!"
- **Horror After Dark**

AVAILABLE IN PRINT, EBOOK, AND AUDIOBOOK

MASS HYSTERIA

MICHAEL PATRICK HICKS

MASS HYSTERIA

It came from space…

Something virulent. Something evil. Something new. And it is infecting the town of Falls Breath.

Carried to Earth in a freak meteor shower, an alien virus has infected the animals. Pets and wildlife have turned rabid, attacking without warning. Dogs and cats terrorize their owners, while deer and wolves from the neighboring woods hunt in packs, stalking and killing their human prey without mercy.

As the town comes under siege, Lauren searches for her boyfriend, while her policeman father fights to restore some semblance of order against a threat unlike anything he has seen before. The Natural Order has been upended completely, and nowhere is safe.

…and it is spreading.

Soon, the city will find itself in the grips of mass hysteria.

To survive, humanity will have to fight tooth and nail.

"Brutal horror. Raw. Animalistic. I couldn't put it down!"
- **Armand Rosamilia, author of the Dying Days series**

"*Mass Hysteria* is a hell of a brutal, end of the world free for all. A terrifying vision of a future gone mad with bloodlust, *Mass Hysteria* will haunt your nightmares."
- **Hunter Shea, author of *Just Add Water* and *We Are Always Watching***

"Fun, horrible fun, from start to finish."
- **Horror Novel Reviews**

AVAILABLE IN PRINT, EBOOK, AND AUDIOBOOK

For more titles and news about future releases,
visit www.michaelpatrickhicks.com and subscribe
to the mailing list.

www.ingramcontent.com/pod-product-compliance
Lightning Source LLC
Chambersburg PA
CBHW032033180726
48284CB00008B/2574